The Pool of Fire

The Pool of Fire

JOHN CHRISTOPHER

G.K. Hall & Co. • Chivers Press
Thorndike, Maine USA   Bath, England

This Large Print edition is published by Thorndike Press, USA and by Chivers Press, England.

Published in 2001 in the U.S. by arrangement with
Simon & Schuster Children's Publishing Division.

Published in 2001 in the U.K. by arrangement with the Author.

U.S. Hardcover ISBN 0-7838-9289-6 (Science Fiction Series Edition)
U.K. Hardcover ISBN 0-7540-4539-0 (Chivers Large Print)

The text of this Large Print edition is unabridged.
Other aspects of the book may vary from the original edition.

Set in 16 pt. Plantin by Al Chase.

Printed in the United States on permanent paper.

British Library Cataloguing-in-Publication Data available

Library of Congress Cataloging-in-Publication Data

Christopher, John.
The pool of fire / John Christopher
p. cm. (The tripods trilogy)
Sequel to: City of gold and lead.
Summary: Will and a small group of free people plan to destroy the three great cities of the Tripods before the arrival of a space ship destined to doom humanity.
ISBN 0-7838-9289-6 (lg. print : hc : alk. paper)
1. Large type books. [1. Science fiction. 2. Large type books.]
I. Title.
PZ7.C457 Po 2001
[Fic]—dc21 00-063191

To my daughter, Elizabeth

Contents

1

A Plan of Action

Everywhere there was the sound of water. In places it was no more than a faint whisper, heard only because of the great stillness all around; in others, an eerie distant rumbling, like the voice of a giant talking to himself in the bowels of the earth. But there were places also where its rushing was clear and loud, and the actual torrent was visible, in the light of oil lamps, flinging itself down dark rocky watercourses or spilling in a fall over a sheer edge of stone. And places where the water lay calm in long black reaches, its sound muted to a monotonous drip . . . drip which had continued for centuries and would continue for as many more.

I was relieved from guard to go to the conference, and so went through the dimly lit tunnels late and alone. The work of nature here mingled with the work of man. The earth's convulsions and the action of long-dead rivers had hollowed out these caverns and channels in the limestone hills, but there were marks of the ancients, too. Men had been here in the past, smoothing uneven floors, widening narrow gaps, sinking handrails into an artificial stone to aid and guide the traveler. There were also long ropelike cables, which had once carried the power called electricity to light bulbs of glass along the way. Our wise men, Beanpole had told me, had learned the means of doing this again, but needed resources that were not available to them here — nor would be, perhaps, while men were forced to skulk like rats in the dark corners of a world governed by the Tripods, those huge metal monsters who strode on three giant legs across the face of the earth.

I have told already how I left my native village, at the urging of a strange man who called himself Ozymandias. This happened during the summer which was to have been my last before I was presented for the Capping ceremony. In that, boys and girls in their fourteenth year were taken up into one of the Tripods and returned later wearing Caps — a metal mesh that fitted close to the skull and made the wearer utterly obedient to our alien rulers. There were always a few whose minds broke under the strain of Capping, and these became Vagrants, men who could not think properly and who wandered aimlessly from place to place. Ozymandias had posed as one of them. In fact, his mission was to recruit people who would fight against the Tripods.

So I went, with my cousin Henry, who also lived in my village, and later with Beanpole, a long journey to the south. (His real name was Jean-Paul, but we nicknamed him Beanpole because he was so tall and thin.) We arrived at last at the White Mountains, where we found the colony of free men Ozymandias had spoken of. From there, the following year, three of us were sent as a spearhead to penetrate into the City from which the Tripods came and learn what we could of them. Not quite the same three, however. Henry was left behind, and in his place we had Fritz, a native of the land of the Germans in which the City stood. He and I had got into the City, served as slaves to the Masters — monstrous three-legged, three-eyed reptilian creatures who came from a distant star — and learned something of their nature and their plans. But only I had escaped, plunging through the drain of the City into a river, and there being rescued by Beanpole. We had waited, hoping Fritz might do the same, until, with snow falling and winter coming on, we had been forced to return, heavy-hearted, to the White Mountains.

We had reached them to find that the colony had moved. This had been the result of a prudent decision by Julius, our leader. He had foreseen the possibility of our being unmasked by the enemy, and of our minds being ransacked once we were helpless in their grasp. So, without telling us of it, he had formed a plan to evacuate the tunnel in the White Mountains, leaving only a few scouts to await our hoped-for return. The scouts had discovered Beanpole and myself as we stared miserably around the deserted fortress, and had led us to the new headquarters.

This lay a long way to the east, in hilly rather than mountainous country. It was a land of narrow valleys, flanked by barren, mostly pine-wooded hills. The Capped kept to the valley floors, we to the ridges. We lived in a series of caves that ran, tortuously, for miles through the heights. Fortunately, there were several entrances. We had guards on them all, and a plan for evacuation in case of attack. But so far all had been quiet. We raided the Capped for food, but were careful to have our raiding parties travel a long way from home before they pounced.

Now Julius had called a conference and I, as the only person who had seen the inside of the City — seen a Master face to face — was summoned from guard duty to attend it.

In the cave where the conference was held, the roof arched up into a darkness that our weak lamps could not penetrate: we sat beneath a cone of night in which no star would ever shine. Lamps flickered from the walls, and there were more on the table, behind which Julius sat with his advisers on roughly carved wooden stools. He rose to greet me as I approached, although any physical action caused him discomfort, if not pain. He had been crippled in a fall as a child, and was an old man now, white-haired but red-cheeked from the long years he had spent in the thin bright air of the White Mountains.

"Come and sit by me, Will," he said. "We are just starting."

It was a month since Beanpole and I had come here. At the outset I had told all I knew to Julius and others of the Council and handed over the things — samples of the Masters' poisonous green air, and water from the City — which I had managed to bring with me. I had expected some kind of swift action, though I did not know what. Swift, I thought, it had to be. One thing I had been able to tell them was that a great ship was on its way, across space, from the home world of the Masters, carrying machines that would turn our earth's atmosphere into air which they could breathe naturally, so that they would not have to stay inside the protective domes of the Cities. Men, and all other creatures native to the planet, would perish as the choking green fog thickened. In four years, my own Master had said, it would arrive, and the machines would be set up. There was so little time.

Julius might have been speaking to me, answering my doubts. He said, "Many of you are impatient, I know. It is right that you should be. We all know how tremendous a task we face, and its urgency. There can be no excuse for action unnecessarily delayed, time wasted. Every day, hour, minute counts.

"But something else counts as much or more; and that is forethought. It is *because* events press so hard on us that we must think and think again before we act. We cannot afford many false moves — perhaps we cannot afford any. Therefore your Council has deliberated long and anxiously before coming to you with its plans. I will give you them in broad detail now, but each one of you has an individual part to play, and that will be told you later."

He stopped, and I saw that someone in the semicircle in front of the table had risen to his feet. Julius said, "Do you wish to speak, Pierre? There will be opportunity later, you know."

Pierre had been on the Council when we first came to the White Mountains. He was a dark, difficult man. Few men opposed Julius, but he had done so. He had, I had learned, been against the expedition to the City of Gold and Lead, and against the decision to move from the White Mountains. In the end, he had left the Council, or been expelled from it; it was difficult to be sure which. He came from the south of France, from the mountains which border on Spanish land. He said, "What I have to say, Julius, is better said first than last."

Julius nodded. "Say it, then."

"You talk of the Council coming to us with its plans. You talk of parts to play, of men being told what they must do. I would remind you, Julius: it is not Capped men you are talking to, but free. You should rather come to us asking than ordering. It is not only you and your Councilors who can plan how to defeat the Tripods. There are others who are not lacking in wisdom. All free men are equal, and must be given the rights of equality. Common sense as well as justice demands this."

He stopped speaking, but remained on his feet, among the more than a hundred men who squatted on the bare rock. Outside it was winter, with even these hills mantled with snow, but, as in the tunnel, we were protected by our thick blanket of rock. The temperature never changed here, from one day or season to another. Nothing changed here.

Julius paused for a moment, before be said, "Free men may govern themselves in different ways. Living and working together, they must surrender some part of their freedom. The difference between us and the Capped is that we surrender it voluntarily, gladly, to the common cause, while their minds are enslaved to alien creatures who treat them as cattle. There is another difference, also. It is that, with free men, what is yielded is yielded for a time only. It is done by consent, not by force or trickery. And consent is something that can always be withdrawn."

Pierre said, "You talk of consent, Julius, but where does your authority lie? In the Council. And who appoints the Council? The Council itself does, under your control. Where is the freedom there?"

"There will be a time," Julius said, "for us to discuss among ourselves how we shall be governed. That day will come when we have destroyed those who now govern humanity all over the world. Until then, we have no room for squabbling or dispute."

Pierre began to say something, but Julius raised a hand and silenced him.

"Nor do we have room for dissension, or the suspicion of dissension. Perhaps what you have said was worth saying, whatever the motive with which you said it. Consent, among free men, is given and can be withdrawn. It can also be affirmed. So I ask: will any man who wishes to challenge the authority of the Council, and its right to speak for this community, rise to his feet?"

He stopped. There was silence in the cave, apart from the shuffle of a foot and the unending distant roar of water. We waited and watched for a second man to get to his feet. None did. When time enough had gone by, Julius said, "You lack support, Pierre."

"Today. But perhaps not tomorrow."

Julius nodded. "You do well to remind me. So I will ask for something else. I ask you now to approve this Council as your government until such a time as those who call themselves the Masters are utterly defeated." He paused. "Will those in favor stand up?"

This time, all stood. Another man, an Italian called Marco, said, "I vote the expulsion of Pierre, for opposing the will of the community."

Julius shook his head. "No. No expulsions. We need every man we have, every man we can get. Pierre will do his part loyally — I know that. Listen. I will tell you what we plan. But first I would like Will here to talk to you of what it is like inside the City of our enemies. Speak, Will."

When I had told my story to the Council, I had

been asked by them to keep silent to others for the time being. Normally this would not have been easy. I am talkative by nature, and my head was full of the wonders I had seen inside the City — the wonders, and the horrors. My mood, though, had not been normal. On the way back, with Beanpole, my energies had been taken up by the arduousness and uncertainty of the journey: there had been little time in which to brood. But after we had come to the caves it had been different. In this world of perpetual lamp-lit night, of echoing silences, I could think and remember, and feel remorse. I found I had no wish to talk to others of what I had seen, and what had happened.

Now, under Julius's instruction to speak, I found myself in confusion. I spoke awkwardly, with many stops and repetitions, at times almost incoherently. But gradually, as I continued with my story, I became aware of how closely they were all listening to it. As I went on, also, I was carried away by my recollection of that terrible time — of what it had been like to struggle under the intolerable burden of the Masters' heavier gravity, sweating in the unvarying heat and humidity, watching fellow slaves weaken and collapse under the strain, and knowing this would almost certainly be my own fate. As it had been Fritz's. I spoke, Beanpole told me later, with passion and with a fluency that was not normally mine. When I had finished and sat down, there was a silence in my audience that told how deeply the story had affected them.

Then Julius spoke again.

"I wanted you to listen to Will for several reasons. One is that what he says is the report of someone who has actually witnessed the things of which he tells. You have heard him, and you know what I mean: what he has described to you he has seen. Another reason is to hearten you. The Masters are possessed of tremendous power and strength. They have traveled the unimaginable distances that lie between the stars. Their lives are so long that ours, by comparison, seem like the dancing of mayflies for a brief day over a tumbling river. And yet . . ."

He paused, and looked at me with a little smile.

"And yet Will, an ordinary boy, no brighter than most, a trifle on the small side — Will has struck at one of these monsters and seen it collapse and die. He was lucky, of course. There is a place where they are vulnerable to a blow, and he was fortunate enough to discover it and to strike there. The fact remains that he killed one of them. They are not all-powerful. We can take heart from that. What Will managed by luck, we can achieve by planning and resolution.

"This leads me to my third point, my third reason for wanting you to hear Will's story. It is that essentially it is a story of failure." He was looking at me, and I felt myself flushing. He went on, calmly and unhurriedly: "The Master was made suspicious by finding in Will's room the notes he had made about the City and its dwellers. Will did not think the Master would go into his room, where he would have to wear a mask to be able to breathe; but this was shallow thinking. After all, he knew his Master was one who took more care of his slaves than most, and knew that he had, before his own time, arranged for small extra comforts to be installed in the refuge room. It was reasonable that he might do so again, and find the book with notes in it."

His tone was level, considering rather than critical, but the more damning for that. My shame and embarrassment grew as I listened to him.

"Will was able, with Fritz's help, to salvage a great deal from the situation. He escaped from the City, and returned with information whose value to us is beyond computing. But still more could have been gained." His eyes were on me again. "And with time to plan things better, Fritz might have come back, too. He passed on to Will as much as he could of what he had learned, but it would have been better if he had been able to testify himself. Because every tiny item counts in the struggle."

Julius spoke then of the short time we had, of the ship already on its way toward us through the far deeps of space, and of the final death for all earthly things which it would bring with it. And he told us what had been decided by the Council.

The most important thing was to speed up —

tenfold, a hundredfold, eventually a thousandfold — our efforts to win the young, those still not Capped, to our side. To do this, as many as possible must go out, winning over and teaching young people, all over the world. Cells of resistance must be set up, and must create other cells. The Council had maps, and would give instructions where to go. Particularly, we must aim at establishing opposition groups in the neighborhood of the other two Cities of the Masters — one thousands of miles across land to the east, the other on the far side of the great ocean to the west. There were problems of language which would have to be overcome. There were other problems — of survival, of organization — which might seem, at first sight, insuperable. They were not insuperable, because they must not be. There could be no weakening, no despair, nothing but a determination to give every last ounce of energy and strength to the cause.

This course, obviously, involved a risk of alerting the Masters to the opposition that was developing. It was possible that they would not bother much about it, since their plan for extermination was so far advanced. But we had to be prepared for countermeasures. We must not have one headquarters, but a dozen, a hundred, each capable of carrying on by itself. The Council would split up, its members traveling from place to place, only meeting occasionally and with due precaution.

So much for the first part of the Plan — the

urgent need to mobilize all available forces for the struggle, and to reconnoiter and set up colonies within reach of all three enemy Cities. There was another part, perhaps even more important. Means had to be devised for destroying them, and this would involve much hard work and experimentation. A separate base was to be set up, but only those allotted to it would know where it was. That was where our ultimate hope lay. We dared not risk its discovery by the Masters.

"Now," Julius said, "I have told you what I can. Later, you will be given your individual instructions, and the things, such as maps, which you may need to carry them out. I will ask now: are there any questions, or suggestions?"

No one spoke, not even Pierre. Julius said, "Then we can go our ways." He paused. "This is the last time we shall meet together, in such an assembly, until our task is completed. The only final thing I would say is what I have said already. That which we have to do is a tremendous and frightening thing, but we must not let it frighten us. It can be done. Yet it can only be done by each one giving his all. Go now, and God go with you."

It was Julius himself who gave me my instructions. I was to travel to the south and east, posing as a trader, with a packhorse, winning recruits and seeding resistance, and reporting back to this center.

Julius asked, "Is it clear to you, Will?"

"Yes, sir."

"Look at me, Will."

I raised my eyes. He said, "I think you are still smarting, lad, from some of the things I said, after you had told your tale to the assembly."

"I realize that what you said was true, sir."

"But that does not make it easier to bear, when one has told a story of courage and skill and high endeavor, and finds it afterward painted a somewhat different color."

I did not answer.

"Listen, Will. What I did, I did for a purpose. The standards we set ourselves must be high, to a point of near impossibility. So I used your story to point a moral: that carelessness, in one man, can destroy us — that enough is never enough — that there can be no complacency, however much is achieved, because there is always more to achieve. But I can tell you now that what you did, you and Fritz, was of tremendous value to us all."

I said, "Fritz did more. And Fritz did not come back."

Julius nodded. "It is a thing you have to suffer. But what matters is that one of you came back — that we did not lose a year out of the brief time we have. We all have to learn to live with our losses, and to use our regrets to spur us on in the future." He put a hand on my shoulder. "It is because I know you that I can say you did well. You will remember it, but you will remember my criticism more clearly and for longer. Isn't that true, Will?"

"Yes, sir," I said. I think it is true."

The three of us — Henry, Beanpole, and I — met at a place we had found where there was a fissure high up in the rock, through which a little weak daylight filtered — just about enough for us to make out each other's faces without the need of lamps. It was some distance from those parts of the caves which were in general use, but we liked going there because of the reminder that the world outside — normally only glimpsed during guard duty at one of the entrances — really did exist: that somewhere there was light and wind and weather, in place of this static blackness and the rumble and whisper and drip of underground water. One day, when there must have been a violent storm blowing outside, a fine mist of rain was driven through the crack and filtered down into our cave. We turned our faces up to it, relishing the cool dampness, and imagining we could smell trees and grass in it.

Henry said, "I'm to go across the western ocean. Captain Curtis is taking us, in the *Orion*. He will pay off his crew in England except for the one who is false-Capped like himself, and those two will sail her down to a port in the west of France, where we shall join them. Six of us. The land we are going to is called America, and the people there speak the English tongue. What about you, Will?"

I told them briefly. Henry nodded, clearly thinking his own the better and more interesting mission. I agreed with him in that; but I did not care much, either.

Henry said, "And you, Beanpole?"

"I don't know where."

"But they've allocated you, surely?"

He nodded. "To the research base."

It was what one should have expected. Beanpole, obviously, was the sort they would need to work things out for the attack against the Masters. The original trio, I thought, really would be split up this time. It did not seem to matter a great deal. My mind was on Fritz. Julius had been quite right: it was what he had said in criticism that I remembered and, remembering, was shamed by. With another week or so to prepare, we might both have escaped. It was my carelessness that had precipitated matters and so led to Fritz being trapped. It was a bitter thought, but inescapable.

The other two were talking, and I was content to let them. They noticed this in time. Henry said, "You're very quiet, Will. Anything wrong?"

"No."

He persisted. "You've been altogether quiet lately."

Beanpole said, "I read a book once about those Americans, to whose land you will be going, Henry. It seems that they have red skins, and go about dressed in feathers, and they carry things like hatchets, and play on drums when they go to war and smoke pipes when they want to be peaceful."

Beanpole was usually too much interested in objects — in the way they worked or could be made to work — to pay any great attention to people. But I realized that he had noticed my unhappiness and guessed the cause of it — after all, he had shared with me the vain wait outside the City, and the journey home — and was doing what he could to distract Henry from questioning and me from brooding. I was grateful for that, and for the nonsense he was talking.

There were many things to do before I could set off. I was instructed in the ways of a packman, taught something of the languages in the countries I would visit, advised on how to set up resistance cells and what to tell them when I moved on. All this I took in conscientiously, and with a determination to make no mistakes this time. But the melancholy I felt did not lift.

Henry left before I did. He went in high spirits, in a party that included Tonio, who had been my sparring partner and rival before we went north to the Games. They were all very cheerful. It seemed that everyone in the caves was, apart from me. Beanpole tried to cheer me up, but without success. Then Julius called me to see him. He gave me a lecture on the futility of self-recrimination, the importance of realizing that the only good lesson to be learned from the past was how to avoid similar errors in the future. I listened, and agreed politely, but the black mood did not lift. He said then, "Will, you are taking this the wrong way. You are someone who does not easily bear criticism, and perhaps least of all from yourself. But to settle into such a mood is something that makes you less capable of doing what the Council requires of you."

"The job will be done, sir," I said. "And properly this time. I promise that."

He shook his head. "I am not sure that such a promise will serve. It would be different if you were of Fritz's temper. Yes, I will speak of him, even though it hurts you. Fritz was melancholic by nature, and could tolerate his own gloom. I do not think this is so with you, who are sanguine and impatient. In your case, remorse and despondency could be crippling."

"I shall do the best I can."

"I know. But will your best be enough?" He looked at me, in slow scrutiny. "You were to have started your journey in three days' time. I think we must delay it."

"But, sir . . ."

"No buts, Will. It is my decision."

I said, "I am ready now, sir. And we do not have the time to waste."

Julius smiled. "There was something of defiance there, so all is not lost. But you are already forgetting what I said at the last assembly. We cannot afford false moves, or plans or people who are not fully prepared. You will stay here a while longer, lad."

I think I hated Julius in that moment. Even when I had got over that, I was bitterly resentful. I watched others leave, and chafed at my own inactivity. The dark sunless days dragged by. I knew that I must change my attitude, but could not. I tried, attempting to put on a false cheerfulness but knowing no one, Julius least of all, was deceived. At last, though, Julius called me back.

He said, "I have been thinking about you, Will. I believe I have found an answer."

"May I go, sir?"

"Wait, wait! As you know, some packmen travel in pairs, for company and so as to protect their goods better from thieves. It might be a good idea for you to have such a companion."

He was smiling. Angry again, I said, "I am well enough by myself, sir."

"But if it is a question of going with another, or staying here — which will you choose?"

It was galling to think that he regarded me as unfit to be sent out on my own. But there was only one answer that it was possible to give. I said, not without sulkiness, "Whatever you decide, sir."

"That's good, Will. The one who is to go with you . . . would you like to meet him now?"

I could see his smile in the lamplight. I said stiffly, "I suppose so, sir."

"In that case . . ." His eyes went to the dark shadows at the edge of the cave, where a row of limestone pillars made a curtain of stone. He called, “You can come forward.”

A figure approached. I stared, thinking that the dimness of the light must be deceiving me. It was easier to disbelieve my eyes than to accept that someone had come back from the dead.

For it was Fritz.

He told me later all that had happened. When he had seen me plunge into the river that led out of the City, under the golden Wall, he had returned and covered my traces as he had said he would, spreading the story that I had found my Master floating in his pool and had gone straightway to the Place of Happy Release, not wishing to live once my Master was dead. It was accepted, and he was ready to make the attempt to follow me out. But the hardships he had suffered, together with the extra exertions of the night we had spent searching for the river, had taken their toll. He collapsed a second time, and a second time was taken to the slaves’ hospital.

It had been agreed that, if I got out, I should wait three days for him to follow. More time than that had passed before he was fit even to rise from his bed, and he thought therefore that I would have gone on. (In fact, Beanpole and I waited twelve days before despair and the coming of the snow drove us away, but Fritz could not know that.) Believing this, he began, as was typical of him, to think the whole thing through again, slowly and logically. He guessed that the underwater plunge through the City’s outlet vents must be difficult — it would have killed me if Beanpole had not been on hand to fish me from the river — and knew the weakness of his own condition. He needed to build up strength, and the hospital offered the best chance of doing that. While he was there, he could avoid his Master's beatings and the heavy tasks that normally were laid on him. He must, of course, be careful not to arouse suspicion that he thought differently from the other slaves, which meant that he had to calculate with care the length of time he could stay. He made it last a fortnight, shamming, for the others, a weakness which increased rather than diminished as the days went by; and then, sorrowfully, declared that he realized he could no longer serve his Master as a Master should be served, and so must die. He left the hospital late in the day, heading toward the Place of Happy Release, found somewhere to hide till night fell, and then made for the Wall and freedom.

At first, all went well. He came out into the river on a dark night, swam wearily to the bank, and went south, following the route we had taken. But he was a couple of days behind us, and fell farther behind when a feverish chill forced him to lie for several days, sweating and starving, in a farmer's barn. He was still desperately weak when he started again, and not long after was halted by a more serious illness. This time, fortunately, he was found and looked after, for he had pneumonia and would have died without care. A lady took him in. Her son, some years before, had turned Vagrant after his Capping. She cherished Fritz because of that.

At last, when he was well and strong, he slipped away and continued his journey. He found the White Mountains swept by blizzards, and was forced to hide out near the valley villages for some time before he could make his way painfully up through deep snow. At the tunnel, he was challenged by the single guard that Julius had left there, just in case. The guard had led him, that morning, to the caves.

All this I learned from him later. At the moment of our meeting, I merely stared, incredulous.

Julius said, "I hope you and your companion will get on together. What do you think, Will?"

Suddenly I realized I was grinning like an idiot.

2

The Hunt

We headed southeast, away from the winter that had closed in over the land. There was a stiff climb, encumbered by drifts of snow, through the mountain pass that took us to the country of the Italians, but after that the going was easier. We traveled across a rich plain, and came to a sea that beat, dark but tideless, against rocky shores and little fishing harbors. So southward, with hills and distant mountains on our left hand, until it was time to break through the heights to the west again.

As peddlers, we were welcomed almost everywhere, not only for the things we brought with us but as new faces in small communities where people, whether liking or disliking them, knew their neighbors all too well. Our wares, to start with, were bolts of cloth, and carvings and small wooden clocks from the Black Forest: our men had captured a couple of barges, trafficking along the great river, and made off with their cargoes. We sold these as we went, and bought other things to sell at a farther stage of our journey. Trade was good; for the most part, these were rich farming lands, the women and children anxious for novelties. The surplus, apart from what we needed to buy food, accumulated in gold and silver coins. And in most places we were given board and lodging. In return for the hospitality we were shown, we stole their boys from them.

This was a thing that I could never properly resolve in my mind. To Fritz, it was simple and obvious: we had our duty, and must do it. Even apart from that, we were helping to save these people from the destruction which the Masters planned. I accepted the logic, and envied him his single-mindedness, but it still troubled me. Part of the difficulty, I think, was that it fell to me more than to him to make friends with them. Fritz, as I now knew well enough, was amiable at heart, but taciturn and withdrawn in appearance. His command of languages was better than my own, but I did more of the talking, and a lot more of the laughing. I quickly got onto good terms with each new community we visited, and moved on, in many cases, with real regret.

Because, as I had learned during my stay in the Château de la Tour Rouge, the fact that a man or a woman wore a Cap, and thought of the Tripods as great metal demigods, did not prevent him or her from being, in all other respects, a likable, even lovable, human being. It was my job to beguile them into accepting us and taking part in our bartering. I did it as well as I could, but I was not able to remain, at the same time, entirely detached. I have always thrown myself into things, unable to hold back, and it was so with this. It was not easy to like them, to recognize their kindness to us, and at the same time to keep to our objective: which was, as they would have seen it, to gain their trust only to betray them. I was often ashamed of what we did.

For our concern was with the young, the boys who would be Capped in the next year or so. We gained their interest in the first case by bribery, giving them small presents of knives, whistles, leather belts, things like that. They flocked around us, and we talked to them, artfully making remarks and putting queries designed to discover which of them had begun to question the right of the Tripods to rule mankind, and to what extent. We rapidly grew skilled at this, developing a good eye for the rebellious, or potentially rebellious.

And there were far more of these than one would have guessed. At the beginning I had been surprised to find that Henry, whom I had known and fought with since we were both able to walk, was as eager as I to break loose from the chafing confinement of life as we knew it — as apprehensive of what our elders told us was the wonderful bliss of being Capped. I had not known, because one did not talk about these things. To voice doubts was unthinkable, but that did not mean that doubts did not exist. It became clear to us that doubts of some kind were in the minds of all those who found the Capping ceremony looming up in their lives. There was an intoxicating sense of release to them in being in the presence of two who seemed to be Capped, yet did not, as their parents did, treat the subject as a mystery that must never he spoken of, but instead encouraged them to talk and listened to what they said.

Of course, we had to be careful in this. It was a matter, at the outset, of veiled hints, inquiries — seemingly innocent — whose effect depended on the look that went with them. Our procedure was to discover the one or two who, in each village, best combined independence of mind and reliability. Then, shortly before we moved on, these were taken to one side, and separately briefed and counseled.

We told them the truth, about the Tripods and the world, and of the part they must play in organizing resistance. It was not a matter now of sending them back to one of our headquarters. Instead, they were to form a resistance group among the other boys in the village or town, and plan an escape before the Spring Cappings. (This would be long enough after our visit for there to be no suspicion that we were concerned in it.) They must find places to live, well apart from the Capped but from where they could raid their lands for food and their youth for new recruits. And where they could wait for new instructions.

There could be little definitely laid down: success must depend on individual skill in improvisation and action. Some small help we could offer, by way of communications. We carried pigeons with us, caged in pairs, and at intervals we left a pair with one of our recruits. These were birds that could return, over vast distances, to the nest from which they had come, and carry messages, written very small on thin paper, tied to their legs. They were to be bred, and their descendants used to keep the various centers in touch with each other and eventually with the headquarters group responsible for them.

We gave them signs of identification, too: a ribbon tied in a horse's mane, hats of a certain kind worn at a certain angle, a way of waving, the simulated cries of certain birds. And places, nearby, where messages could be left, to guide us again, or our successors, to whatever hiding place they had found. Beyond that, we could do no more than leave it in the hand of Providence; and go our way, farther and farther, on the path Julius had prescribed for us.

At the beginning, we had seen Tripods fairly frequently. As we went on, though, this happened less and less. It was not a matter of the winter making them inactive, we found, but a real effect of distance from the City. In the land called Hellas, we were told that they appeared only a few times in the year, and in the eastern parts of that country the villagers told us that the Tripods came only for the Capping ceremonies, and then not to every small place, as they did in England: children were brought great distances by their parents to be Capped.

This was reasonable, of course. The Tripods

could travel fast — many times the speed of a galloping horse — and without stopping, but distance must take its toll even of them. It was inevitable that they should police those regions close to the City more thoroughly than far-off places: each mile represented a widening of the circle of which it was the center. For our part, it was a relief to find ourselves in territories where we could be well nigh certain — at this time of year — that no metal hemisphere on its three jointed legs would break the skyline. And it raised a thought. There were two Cities of the Masters, at either edge, more or less, of this vast continent. If control grew more tenuous the farther one traveled from a City, might there not be a part, midway between them, where control did not exist at all — where men were un-Capped and free?

(In fact, as we learned later, the arcs of control overlapped each other, and the area falling outside them was mostly ocean in the south and wastes of frozen land in the north. Those lands, farther to the south, which they did not control, they had laid waste.)

Our task did not, as one might have thought, become easier where the Tripods were less familiar. If anything they seemed, perhaps through their rarity, to inspire a more complete devotion. We reached a land at last, beyond an isthmus between two seas, near which stood the ruins of a great-city (it was relatively little overgrown with vegetation, but looked far more ancient than any other we had seen), in which there were great hemispheres of wood, set on three stilts and approached by steps, in which the people worshiped. Long, involved services were conducted there, with much chanting and wailing. Above each hemisphere stood a model of a Tripod, gold not with paint but with the beaten leaf of the metal itself.

But we persisted, and found converts there, also. We were becoming more skilled at our job by this time.

There were tribulations, of course. Although we had moved south, into sunnier, warmer lands, there were times of bitter cold, particularly in the higher regions, when we had to huddle close to the horses at night to keep the blood from freezing in our veins. And long arid days, in near-desert regions, when we had to look anxiously for a sign of water, not so much for ourselves as for the horses. We depended on them absolutely, and it was a staggering blow when Fritz's horse sickened and, a couple of days later, died. I was selfish enough to be glad that it was not my own horse, Crest, of whom I was very fond — if Fritz felt anything of that sort he kept it firmly to himself — but even more concerned with the difficulties that faced us.

We were in bad country, too, on the edge of a great desert and a long way from habitation. We transferred as much of our baggage as possible to Crest, and plodded off, walking now of course, in the direction of the nearest village. As we went, we saw large ugly birds drop from the lazy circles they had been making in the sky to rip the flesh from the poor beast's bones. They would be picked clean within an hour.

This was in the morning. We traveled all that day and half of the next before we reached a few stone huts clustering about an oasis. There was no hope of replacing our lost animal there and we had to trek on, another three days, to what was described as a town, though no bigger in fact than the village of Wherton, where I was born. Here there were animals, and we had the gold we had collected with which to pay for one. The difficulty was that horses, in these parts, were never used as beasts of burden, but only as gaudily caparisoned steeds for persons of high rank. We could not have afforded to buy one, and would have bitterly offended local custom if we had done so and then put packs on it.

What they did have here was a creature whose picture I had once seen, on the side of a carton which I had found in the tunnel that led up through the White Mountains; and gazed at curiously, as an inexplicable relic of the ancients. Now I saw it in the life. It was covered in coarse light brown hair and stood higher than a horse, and had a huge hump on its back which we were told contained a store of water on which it could live for days, a week even, if necessary. Instead of hoofs it had great splayed feet with toes. The head, at the end of a long neck, was hideously ugly, with loose lips and big yellow teeth and, I may say, foul breath. The animal looked awkward and ungainly, but could move surprisingly fast and carry huge loads.

Fritz and I had a disagreement in regard to this. I wanted us to purchase one of these beasts, and he opposed it. I suffered the usual frustration that took place when we were at odds over something. My passionate statement of my own argument was met by stolid unyielding resistance on his part. This made me indignant — my indignation made him more sullenly obstinate — which increased my indignation further . . . and so on. My enumeration of the animal's advantages was answered by the simple counter that we had almost reached the point at which we should turn and start our return swing toward the caves. However useful it might be in these parts, it would look bizarre in places where it was not familiar, and the one thing we must not do was attract undue attention. It was also likely, Fritz pointed out, that, being accustomed to this particular climate, it might well sicken and die in more northerly lands.

He was, of course, quite right, but we spent two days wrangling before I could bring myself to admit it. And to admit, to myself at least, that it was the very bizarreness which had in part, attracted me. I had been envisaging myself (poor Crest forgotten for the moment) riding through the streets of strange towns on the creature's swaying back, and people flocking around to stare at it.

With same amount of money we were able to buy two donkeys — small, but hardy and willing beasts — and loaded our goods on them. We also had enough to purchase the wares of this country: dates, various spices, silks, and finely woven carpets, which we sold very profitably later on. But we made few converts. The language defeated us both utterly. We could buy and sell and barter in sign language, but one required words to talk of liberty and the need to win it from those who enslaved us. Also, the cult of the Tripods was far stronger here. The hemispheres were everywhere, the larger ones having a platform under the Tripod figure at the top, from which a priest called the faithful to prayer three times a day, at dawn and noon and sunset. We bowed our heads and muttered with the rest.

So we reached the river indicated on our map, a broad warm waterway which moved in sluggish serpentine coils through a green valley. And turned back toward home.

The return journey was different. We took a pass through a range of mountains and came out near the eastern shore of that sea we had glimpsed from the ruined great-city that stood on the isthmus. We followed it around, to the north and west, making good time and once more winning great numbers to our cause. The people spoke the Russian tongue, and we had been given some instruction in this, and notes to study. We traveled north, but summer was outstripping us: the land was bright with flowers and I recall one time when we rode all day long in the intoxicating scent of young oranges, ripening on the branches of huge groves of trees. Our schedule called for us to be back at the caves before winter, and we had to press on fast to keep it.

We were moving back toward the City of the Masters as well, of course. From time to time, we saw Tripods, striding across the horizon. We saw none close at hand, though, and were grateful for that. None, that is, until the Day of the Hunt.

The Masters, as we had learned, treated the Capped differently in different places. I do not know whether the spectacle of human variety amused them — they themselves, of course, had always been of one race and the notions of national differences, of many individual languages, of war, which had been the curse of mankind before their conquest, were utterly strange to them. In any case, although they prohibited war they encouraged other forms of diversity and separateness, and cooperated to some extent in human customs. Thus, in the Capping ceremony, they followed a ritual, as their slaves did, appearing at a certain time, sounding a particular dull booming call, fulfilling prescribed motions. At the tournaments in France, and at the

Games, they attended patiently throughout, though their only direct interest was in the slaves they would acquire at the end. Perhaps, as I say, this sort of thing amused them. Or perhaps they felt that it fulfilled their role as gods. At any rate, we came to a strange and horrible demonstration of it, when we were only a few hundred miles from our journey's end.

For many days we had been following a vast river, on which, as in the case of the river that had led us north to the Games, much traffic plied. Where the ruins of a great-city lay in our path, we detoured onto higher ground. The land was well cultivated, to a large extent with vines which had been recently stripped of grapes for the harvest. It was well populated, and we stayed the night at a town that looked down toward the ruins and the river and the broad plain beyond, through which it ran into an autumn sunset.

The town, we found, was seething with excitement, crowded with visitors from as much as fifty miles around, on account of what was to take place the following day. We asked questions, as ignorant wandering peddlers, and were answered readily enough. What we learned was horrifying.

The day was called by different names — some spoke of the Hunt, others of Execution Day.

In my native England, murderers were hanged, a brutal and disgusting thing but one which was thought necessary to protect the innocent, and which was carried out expeditiously and as humanely as such a practice could be. Here, instead, they were kept in prison until one day in the autumn, when the grapes were in and pressed and the first new wine ready. Then a Tripod came, and one by one the condemned were turned loose, and the Tripod hunted them while the townspeople watched and drank wine and cheered the sight. Tomorrow there were four to be hunted and killed, a greater number than there had been for several years. On that account the excitement was the greater. The new wine would not be served until the morrow, but there was old wine enough and a good deal of drunkenness as they slaked their thirsts and soothed their fevered anticipations.

I turned from the sight, sickened, and said to Fritz, "At least we can leave at daybreak. We do not have to stay and watch what happens."

He looked at me calmly. "But we must, Will."

"Watch a man, whatever his crime, sent out for a Tripod to course him like a hare? While his fellow men make wagers on the time he will last?" I was angry and showed it. "I do not call that an entertainment."

"Nor do I. But anything which concerns the Tripods is important. It is as it was when we were in the City together. Nothing must be overlooked."

"You do it, then. I will go on to the next halt, and wait for you there."

"No." He spoke tolerantly but firmly. "We were instructed to work together. Besides, between here and the next village, Max might put his foot in a hole and throw me and I might break my neck in the fall."

Max and Moritz were the names he had given the two donkeys, after characters in certain stories that German boys were told in their childhood. We both smiled at the thought of the sure-footed Max putting a foot wrong. But I realized that there was a lot in what Fritz said: witnessing the scene was part of our job and not to be shirked on account of its unpleasantness.

"All right," I said. "But we move on the moment it's over. I don't want to stay in this town any longer than I have to."

He looked around the café in which we were sitting. Men sang drunkenly and banged their glasses on the wooden tables, spilling wine. Fritz nodded.

"I, neither."

The Tripod came during the night. In the morning it stood like a huge sentinel in a field just below the town, silent, motionless, as those other Tripods had stood at the tournament of the Tour Rouge and at the Games Field. This was a day of festival. Flags were flown, lines of bunting ran from roof to roof across the narrow streets, and street traders were out early, selling hot sausages, sweetmeats, sandwiches of chopped raw meat and onion, ribbons and trinkets. I looked at a tray one man was carrying. It contained a dozen or more little wooden Tripods, each holding in a tentacle the tiny agonized figure of a man. The trader was a cheerful, red-faced fellow and I saw another as kindly looking, a prosperous gaitered farmer with a bushy white beard, buy two of them for his twin grandchildren, a flaxen-headed boy and pigtailed girl of six or seven.

There was much competition for the good vantage points. I did not feel like pressing for one of these, but Fritz, in any case, had fixed things. Many householders, whose windows looked down from the town, rented space at them, and he had bought places for us. The charge was high, but it included free wine and sausages. It also included the use of magnifying glasses.

I had seen a shop window full of these, and had gathered that this was a center for their manufacture. I had wondered why at the time, not understanding the connection. I knew now. We looked out over the heads of a crowd, with the sunlight glinting from a great number of lenses. Not far away, where a road ran steeply downhill, a man had set up a telescope on a stand. It was at least six feet long, and he was shouting, "Genuine close-up views! Fifty groschen for ten seconds! Ten schillings for the kill! As close as if he were on the other side of the street!"

The crowd's frenzy grew with the waiting. Men stood on platforms and took bets — as to how long the Hunt would last, how far the man would get. This seemed absurd to me at first, for I did not see how he could get any distance at all.

But one of the others in the room explained things. The man was not sent out on foot, but on horseback. The Tripod could easily outdistance the horse, of course, but a horseman, taking what advantage he could of the terrain, might evade being taken for as long as a quarter of an hour.

I asked if anyone ever escaped entirely. My companion shook his head. It was theoretically possible: there was a rule that beyond the river there was no pursuit. But it had never happened, in all the years that the Hunt had been held.

Suddenly the crowd hushed. I saw that a saddled horse was being led into the field above which the Tripod loomed. Men in gray uniform brought another man there, dressed in white. I stared through the glasses and saw that he was a tall, rawboned man, about thirty, who looked lost and bewildered. He was helped to mount the horse, and sat there, with the uniformed men holding the stirrups on either aide. The hush deepened. Into it came the tolling of the bell of the church clock, as it struck the hour of nine. On the last stroke they stood back, slapping the horse's flank. The horse bounded forward, and the crowd's voice rose in a cry of recognition and exultation.

He rode down the slope toward the distant silver gleam of the river. He had gone perhaps a quarter of a mile before the Tripod moved. A huge metal foot uprooted itself, soared through the sky, and was followed by another. It was not hurrying particularly. I thought of the man on horseback, and felt his fear rise as bile in my own mouth. I looked from the scene to the faces around me. Fritz's was impassive, as usual, intent and observing. The others . . . they nauseated me, I think, more than what was taking place outside.

It did not last long. The Tripod got him as he galloped across the bare brown slope of a vineyard. A tentacle came down and picked him from the horse with the neatness and sureness of a girl threading a needle. Another cry rose from those who watched. The tentacle held him, a struggling doll. And then a second tentacle . . .

My stomach heaving, I scrambled to my feet, and ran from the room.

The atmosphere was different when I returned, the feverishness having been replaced by a sort of relaxation. They were drinking wine and talking about the Hunt. He had been a poor specimen, they decided. One, who appeared to be a senior servant from the estate of a count who had a castle nearby, had lost money on him and was indignant about it. My reappearance was greeted with a few mocking remarks and some laughter. They told me I was a weak-bellied foreigner, and urged me to have a liter of wine to steady my nerves. Outside, the same relaxation — a sense almost of repletion — could be observed in the crowd. Bets were being paid off, and there was a brisk trade in hot pastries and sweetmeats. The Tripod, I noticed, had gone back to its original position in the field.

Gradually, as the hour ticked by, tension built up once more. At ten o'clock, the ceremony repeated itself, with the same quickening of excitement in those about us, the same roar of joy and approval as the Hunt began. The second victim gave them better sport. He rode fast and well, and for a time avoided the Tripod's tentacle by riding under the cover of trees. When he broke into the open again, I wanted to shout to him to stay where he was. But it would have done no good, as he must have known: the Tripod could have plucked the trees out from around him. He was making for the river, and I saw that there was another copse half a mile farther on. Before he got there, the tentacle swept down. The first time he dodged it, swerving his horse at just the right moment so that the rope of metal flailed down and hit the ground beside him. He had a chance, I thought, of reaching his objective, and the river was not so very much farther on. But the Tripod's second attempt was better aimed. He was plucked from the saddle and his body pulled apart, as the first man's had been. In a sudden hush, his cries of agony came thinly to us through the bright autumnal air.

I did not come back after that killing. There were limits to what I could stand, even in the cause of duty. Fritz stuck it out, but he looked grim when I saw him later, and was even more taciturn than usual.

A few weeks later, we reached the caves. Their gloomy depths were strangely attractive, a haven from the world through which we had journeyed for almost a year. The walls of rock enfolded us, and the lamps flickered warmly. More important, though, was the release from the strain of mixing with and dealing with the Capped. Here we conversed with free men like ourselves.

For three days we were idle, apart from the ordinary duties which all shared. Then we had our orders from the local commander, a German whose name was Otto. We were to report, in two days' time, at a place specified only as a point on a map. Otto himself did not know why.

3

The Green Man on the Green Horse

It took us two full days, on horseback, riding hard for the most part. Winter was closing in again fast, the days shortening, a long fine spell of St. Luke's summer breaking up into cold unsettled weather coming from the west. For the whole of one morning we rode with sleet and sharp rain driving into our faces. We slept the first night in a small inn, but as the second day drew to its close we were in wild deserted country, with sheep cropping thin grass and not even a sign of a shepherd, or a shepherd's hut.

We were, we knew, near the end of our journey. At the top of a slope we reined in our horses and looked down to the sea, a long line beating against an unpromising rocky coast. All empty, as the land was. Except . . . Away to the north, on the very edge of visibility, something like a squat finger pointing upward. I spoke to Fritz, and he nodded, and we rode for it.

As we got nearer, we could see that it was the ruin of a castle, set on a promontory of rock. Nearer still, we could make out that there had been a small harbor on the far side and that there were more ruins there, though on a more modest scale. Fishermen's cottages, most likely. It would have been a fishing village once, but was now abandoned. We saw no indication of life, either there or in the castle, which loomed harsh and black against the deepening gray sky. A broken, potholed road led up to a gateway from which, on one side, hung the shattered remnants of a wooden gate barred with iron. Riding through, we found ourselves in a courtyard.

It was as empty and lifeless as everything else, but we dismounted, and tied our horses to an iron ring that had, perhaps, been used for that very purpose a thousand years before. Even if we had got our map reference wrong, we were going to have to leave the search until morning. But I could not believe we had erred. From behind an embrasure, I saw a dim flicker of light, and touched Fritz's arm, pointing. It disappeared, and was visible again farther along the wall. I could just make out that there was a door and that the light was moving in that direction. We went toward it, and reached it as a figure, carrying a lamp, turned a corner in the corridor within. He held the lamp higher, shining it in our faces.

"You're a bit late," he said. "We'd given you up for today."

I went forward with a laugh. I still could not see his face, but I knew well enough whose voice it was! Beanpole's.

Certain rooms (those facing seaward, for the most part) and a section of the dungeons had been refurbished and made habitable. We were given a good hot supper, of rich stew, followed by home-baked bread and French cheese, wheel-shaped, dusted white outside, creamy yellow within, strong-tasting and satisfying. There was hot water to wash ourselves, and beds had been made up in one of the spare rooms, with sheets. We slept well, lulled by the roar and rumble of the sea breaking on the rocks, and awoke refreshed. For breakfast, there were others present, as well as Beanpole. I recognized two or three faces that I had known as belonging to that group which studied the wisdom of the ancients. Someone else who was familiar came in while we were eating. Julius hobbled across the room toward us, smiling.

"Welcome, Fritz. And Will. It's good to see you back with us again."

We had asked questions of Beanpole, and received evasive answers. All would be explained in the morning, he told us. And after breakfast we went, with Julius and Beanpole and half a dozen others, to a huge room on the castle's first floor. There was a great gaping window looking out to sea, across which a frame of wood and glass had been fastened, and an altogether enormous fireplace in which wood crackled and burned. We sat down on benches behind a long, rough-hewn table, in no particular order. Julius spoke to us.

"I shall satisfy the curiosity of Will and Fritz first," he said. "The rest of you must bear with me." He looked at us. "This is one of several places at which research into ways of defeating the Masters is being carried out. Many ideas have been put forward, many of them ingenious. All have drawbacks, though, and the chief drawback, common to every one, is that we still, despite the reports you two made, know so little about our enemy."

He paused for a moment. "A second trio was sent north to the Games last summer. Only one qualified to be taken into the City. We have heard nothing more of him. He may yet escape — we hope he will — but we cannot depend on that. In any case, it is doubtful that he could give us the information we want. Because what we really need, it has been decided, is one of the Masters in our hands, alive for preference, so that we can study him."

My face may have shown my skepticism; I have always heard it shows too much. At any rate, Julius said, "Yes, Will, an impossible requirement, one would think. But perhaps not quite impossible. This is why you two have been called in to help us. You have actually seen the inside of a Tripod, when you were being taken to the City. You have, it is true, described it to us already, and fully. But if we are going to capture a Master, we must get him out of that metal stronghold in which he strides about our lands. And for that, the smallest recollection which you may be able to dredge from your memories could be of help."

Fritz said, "You talk of taking one alive, sir. But how can that be done? Once he is out of the Tripod, he will choke, within seconds, in our atmosphere."

"A good point," Julius said, "but we have an answer to it. You brought back samples from the City. We have learned how to reproduce the green air in which they live. A room has already been prepared here in the castle, sealed and with an air lock to enable us to pass in and out."

Fritz said, "But if you manage to bring a Tripod here, and wreck it here . . . the others will come looking for it. They can destroy the castle easily enough."

"We also have a box big enough to hold one of them, and can seal that. If we make the capture farther along the coast, we can bring him here by boat."

I said, "And the means of capturing, sir? I would not have thought that was easy."

"No," Julius agreed, "not easy. But we have been studying them. They are creatures of routine, and generally follow particular paths. We have mapped and timetabled many of them. There is a place, some fifty miles to the north, where one passes every nine days. It strides across rough commonland at the sea's edge. Between one passing and the next we have nine days to dig a hole and cover it lightly with brush and clods. We will bring our Tripod down, and after that all we have to do is winkle the Master out and get him into his box and onto the boat lying hard by. From what you and Fritz told us — that their breathing is much slower than ours — there should be no danger of his suffocating before we can get a mask on him."

Fritz objected, "They can communicate with each other, and with the City, by invisible rays."

Julius smiled. "We can handle that part, too. Now, talk to us about the Tripods. There is paper in front of you, and pencils. Draw diagrams of them. Drawing will refresh your memories also."

We were a week at the castle before moving north. During that time I learned a little, from Beanpole and the others, of the great strides that had been taken, during the previous year, in relearning the skills of the ancients. A breakthrough had been made by an expedition into the ruins of one of the great-cities, where a library had been found containing thousands on thousands of books which explained the marvels of the time before the Tripods came. These gave access to an entire world of knowledge. It was possible now, Beanpole told me, to make those bulbs which, by means of the power called electricity, would glow with light far brighter and more constant than the oil lamps and candles to which we were accustomed. It was possible to get heat from an arrangement of wires, to build a carriage which would travel along not pulled by horses but by means of a small engine inside it. I looked at Beanpole, when he said that.

"Then the Shmand-Fair could be made to work again, as it used to work?"

"Very easily. We know how to machine metals, to make the artificial stone which the ancients called concrete. We could put up towering buildings, create great-cities again. We can send messages by the invisible rays that the Masters use — even send pictures through the air! There is so much that we can do, or could learn to do in a short time. But we are concentrating only on those things which are of direct and immediate help in defeating the enemy. For instance, at one of our laboratories we have developed a machine which uses great heat to cut through metal. It will be waiting for us in the north."

Laboratories, I wondered — what were they? My mind was confused by much of what he said. We had both learned a lot during the time we had been separated, but his knowledge was so much greater and more wonderful than mine. He looked a lot older. The ridiculous contraption of lenses, which he had worn when we first set eyes on him, at the other side of the smoky bar in the French fishing town, had been replaced by a neat symmetrical affair which sat on the bridge of his long thin nose and gave him an air of maturity and authority. They were called spectacles, he had told me, and others among the scientists wore them. Spectacles, scientists . . . so many words, describing things outside my ken.

I think he realized how much at a loss I felt. He

asked me questions about my own experiences, and I told him what I could. He listened to it all intently, as though my ordinary travels were as interesting and important as the fantastic things he had been learning and doing. My heart warmed to him for that.

We set up camp in caves not far from the intended place of ambush. The boat we were to use, a forty-foot fishing smack, stayed close at hand, her nets out to provide an appearance of innocence. (In fact, she caught a fair haul of fish, mostly mackerel; some provided rations for us and the rest were thrown back.) On a particular morning, we kept well out of sight while two of our number went farther up, to hide behind rocks and watch the Tripod pass. Those of us who stayed in the cave heard it, anyway: it was making one of the calls whose meaning we did not know, an eerie warbling sound. As it faded in the distance, Julius said, "On time, to the minute. Now we start to work."

We labored hard at preparing the trap. Nine days was not so long a time, when it involved digging away enough earth to serve as a pitfall for a thing with fifty-foot legs, leaving a pattern of supports on which the camouflage must rest. Beanpole, pausing in his digging, spoke wistfully of something which had been called a bulldozer, and which could move earth and stones by the ton. But that was another thing there had not been time enough to recreate.

At any rate, we got through the task, with a day to spare. The day seemed longer than the previous eight had. We sat in the mouth of the cave, looking out to a gray, calm, cold sea, patched with mist. At least, the sea journey should not offer much difficulty. Once we had trapped our Tripod, and caught our Master, that was.

The weather stayed cold and dry next morning. We took up our places — all of us this time — an hour before the Tripod was due to pass. Fritz and I were together, Beanpole with the man working the jammer. This was a machine that could send out invisible rays of its own, to break up the rays coming to and going from the Tripod and isolate it, for the time being, from any contact with the others. I was full of doubts about this, but Beanpole was very confident. He said these rays could be interrupted by natural things like thunderstorms: the Masters would think something like that had happened, until it was too late to do anything about it.

The minutes and seconds crawled by. Gradually my concentration turned into a sort of daze. I was jolted back to reality by Fritz silently touching my shoulder. I looked and saw the Tripod swing around the side of a hill to the south, heading directly for us. Immediately I tensed, in body and mind, for the part I was to play. It was traveling at an average speed. In less than five minutes . . . Then, without warning, the Tripod stopped. It halted with one of its three feet raised, looking absurdly like a dog begging for a bone. For three or four seconds it stayed there. The foot came down. The Tripod continued its progress; but it was no longer heading our way. It had changed course, and would miss us by a couple of miles at least.

In stunned amazement, I watched it travel on and disappear. From behind a clump of trees on the other side of the pitfall, André, our leader, came out and waved. We went to join him, along with the others.

It was soon established what had gone wrong. The Tripod's hesitation had coincided with the ray jammer being turned on. It had stopped, and then shied away. The man who had worked the machine said, "I should have waited till it was on top of the trap. I didn't expect it to react like that."

Someone asked, "What do we do now?"

The let-down feeling was apparent in all of us. All the work and waiting for nothing. It made our entire project, of overthrowing the Masters, seem hopeless, childlike almost.

Julius had come hobbling up. He said, "We wait, of course." His calmness was steadying. "We wait till next time, and then we don't use the jammer until the absolutely last moment. Meanwhile, we can extend the trap farther still."

So the working and waiting went on, for nine more days, and zero hour came around again. The Tripod appeared, as it had done previously, marched around the side of the hill, reached the point where it had stopped the time before. This time it did not stop. But it did not come on toward us, either. Without hesitation, it took the identical course it had taken after its earlier check. Seeing it go, well out of our reach, was more than a double bitterness.

Holding a council of war, we were in low spirits. Even Julius, I thought, was dismayed, though he did his best not to show it. I found it quite impossible to conceal my own despair.

Julius said, "One sees how it works. They follow set courses on these patrols. If the course is varied for some reason, the variation is kept on subsequent trips."

A scientist said, "It probably has something to do with automatic piloting." I wondered what that was. "The course is plotted — and if you override it you set up a new pattern which remains constant unless that is overridden in turn. I see the mechanism of it."

Which was more than I did. Talking about the why and wherefore did not strike me as important. The question was; how to get at the Tripod now?

Someone suggested digging another pitfall, across the new course. The remark fell into silence, which Julius broke.

"We could do that. But it does not pass within two miles of the shore, and the going in between is very bad. No road, not even a track. I think we should have them swarming around us before we had got our prisoner half the distance to the boat."

The silence was resumed, and lengthened. After some seconds, André said, "I suppose we could call this operation off temporarily. We could find another track within reach of the sea, and work on that instead."

Someone else said, "It took us four months to find this one. Finding another could take us as long, or longer."

And every day counted: none of us needed telling that. Silence fell again. I tried to think of something, but discovered only a hopeless blank in my mind. There was a sharp wind, and a smell of snow in the air. Land and sea alike were black and desolate, under a lowering sky. It was Beanpole who spoke at last. He said, diffident in the presence of our elders, "It does not seem that the jamming last week made it suspicious. It would hardly have come so close again if so; or would have come closer yet, to investigate. The altered course is — well, more or less an accident."

André nodded. "That seems to be true. Does it help?"

"If we could lure it back onto the old course . . ."

"An excellent idea. The only problem is: how? What is there that will lure a Tripod? Do you know? Does anyone?"

Beanpole said, "I am thinking of something Will told me that Fritz and he witnessed."

He told them, briefly, the story I had told him

about the Hunt. They listened, but when he had finished, one of the scientists said, "We know of this. It happens in other places, as well. But it's a tradition, and caused as much by the Capped as by the Tripods. Do you suggest we start a tradition during the next nine days?"

Beanpole started to say something, which was interrupted. All our nerves were frayed; tempers likely to be short. Julius, though, cut across the interruption, "Go on, Jean-Paul."

He sometimes stammered a little when he was nervous, and did so now. But the impediment disappeared as he warmed up to what he was saying.

"I was thinking . . . we know they are curious about strange things. When Will and I were floating downriver on a raft . . . one of them veered off course and smashed the raft with its tentacle. If someone could attract this one's attention, and perhaps lead it *into* the trap . . . I think it might work."

It might, at that. André objected. "To attract attention, and then stay out of its clutches long enough to bring it to us . . . it sounds like a tall order."

"On foot," Beanpole said, "it would be impossible. But, in the Hunt that Will and Fritz saw, the men were on horseback. One lasted for quite a long time, covering a distance as great as the one we want or more, before he was caught."

There was a pause again, as we considered what he had said. Julius said thoughtfully, "It might work. But can we be quite sure he will rise to the bait? As you say, they are curious about strange things. A man on horseback . . . They see them every day by the score."

"If the man were dressed in something bright — and perhaps the horse painted . . ."

"Green," Fritz said. "It is their own color, after all. A green man on a green horse. I think that would attract attention, all right."

There was a murmur of approval of the idea. Julius said, "I like that. Yes, it could do. All we need now is our horse and rider."

I felt excitement rise in me. They were mostly scientists, unused to such humdrum physical pursuits as horse riding. The two with the obviously best claim were Fritz and I. And Crest and I had grown used to and skilled in understanding one another through a long year's journeying.

I said, catching Julius's eye, "Sir, if I might suggest . . ."

We used a green dye on Crest, which would wash off afterward. He took the indignity well, with only a snort or two of disgust. The color was bright emerald, and looked startling. I wore a jacket and trousers of the same eye-wrenching hue. I objected when Beanpole approached my face with a rag dipped in the die but, on Julius's confirmation, submitted, Fritz, looking on, burst into laughter. He was not much given to mirthfulness, but then, I suppose, he was not often treated to so comic a spectacle.

During the previous nine days I had rehearsed and re-rehearsed my part in this morning's events. I was to pick up the Tripod as it came around the hill and, as soon as it made a move in my direction, gallop at full speed for the pitfall. We had fixed a narrow causeway over the top, which we hoped would take Crest's weight and mine, and marked it with signs which were meant to be conspicuous enough for me to see and yet unlikely to attract suspicion on the part of the Masters in the Tripod. The latter had seemed the greater risk, so we had erred on the side of caution. It was a tenuous and ill-defined path I had to follow, and three or four times we had found ourselves off course and only saved by a last-minute swerve from plunging into the pit below.

Now, at last, all was ready; with preparations made and only requiring to be translated into action. I checked Crest's girths for the tenth time. The others shook hands with me, and withdrew. I was very lonely as I watched them go. Now there was the waiting again, familiar yet unfamiliar. This time it was more crucial, and this time I was alone.

I felt it first: the earth beneath us vibrating to the distant stamp of the huge metal feet. Another, and another — a steady succession of them, each more audible than the one before. I had Crest's head pointed in the direction of the pitfall, with my own head twisted around to the right, watching for the Tripod. It came, a monstrous leg breaking the line of the hill, followed by the hemisphere. I shivered, and felt Crest shiver, as well. I did my best to pat him back into calm. I was on the alert for any deviation from the course the Tripod had now followed on two occasions. If it did not move toward me, I must move toward it. I hoped I would not have to. It would take me farther away from the pitfall and mean also that I had to turn to lead it there, both procedures which would make the enterprise that much more perilous.

Its course changed. It did not break step, but one of the legs swung around. I wasted no more time, but touched my heels to Crest's sides. He shot off, and the chase was on.

I wanted to look back, to see how my pursuer was closing on me, but dared not; every scrap of energy had to go into the gallop. I could tell, though, by the shortening of the intervals between footfalls, that the Tripod was increasing speed. Landmarks familiar from my practice runs fell away on either side. Ahead there was the coast, the sea dark gray but capped with white from a freshening wind. The wind blew in my face, and I felt an absurd resentment against it for slowing, even by a fraction of a fraction of a second, my flight. I passed a thornbush I knew, a rock shaped like a cottage loaf. No more than a quarter of a mile to go . . . And as I framed the thought, I heard the whistling of steel through the air, the sound of the tentacle swishing down toward me.

I made a guess, and urged Crest to the right. I thought I had got away with it this time — that the tentacle would miss — then felt Crest shudder violently with the shock of being hit by the metal flail. It must have caught him on the hindquarters, just behind the saddle. He swayed and collapsed. I managed to get my feet out of the stirrups and went forward over his head as he fell. I hit the ground rolling, scrambled to my feet, and ran.

At every instant I expected to be plucked up into the air. But the Master controlling the Tripod was more immediately concerned with Crest. I saw him, as I glanced quickly back, lifted, struggling feebly, and brought within closer view of the green ports at the bottom of the hemisphere. I dared not pay any more attention to him, but ran on. A couple of hundred yards only . . . If the Tripod concentrated on Crest long enough, I was there.

I risked glancing back again just in time to see my poor horse dropped, from a height of sixty feet, to land in a broken heap on the ground; and to see the Tripod begin to move again in a new pursuit. I could run no faster than I was running already. The metal feet thudded after me, the edge of the pitfall seemed to get no nearer. For the last fifty yards I thought I was finished, that the tentacle was on the point of reaching for me. I think perhaps the Master was playing with me, like a great steel cat with a scurrying mouse. That was what Beanpole suggested afterward.

All I knew then was that my legs were aching, my lungs, it seemed, on the point of bursting. I became aware, as I reached the pitfall, of a new hazard. I had learned the trail across from horseback height and things were different to a running man: the change in perspective was utterly confusing. At the last moment, I recognized a certain stone and made for it. I was on the causeway. But I still had to get across, and the Tripod had to follow me.

I knew that it had done so — that I had succeeded in my task — when, in place of the stamp of a foot on solid ground, I heard a ripping, tearing noise behind me, and at the same time felt the surface beneath my feet change and collapse. I grabbed wildly at a length of branch which had been knitted into the camouflaged surface of the pit. It came away, and I was falling again. I seized another branch, of thorn this time, and it held longer, lacerating my hands as I gripped it. While I was suspended like this the sky darkened above me. The pit's surface had given way beneath the foremost leg of the Tripod, with the second leg in midair. Off balance, it was plunging forward, the hemisphere swinging helplessly across and down. Looking up, I saw it pass me and a moment later heard the shock of its impact with the solid ground on the far side of the pit. I myself was hanging halfway up the pit, at grave risk of falling the rest of the way. No one, I knew, was going to come to my assistance; they all had more important work to do. I set myself to collect my scattered senses and to climb, slowly and gingerly, up the network of reeds and branches on which I was suspended.

By the time I reached the scene, things were well underway. There was no external seal on the compartment which was used to transport human beings, as we had been transported from the Games field to the City, and the circular door had, in fact, fallen open with the shock. Fritz guided the team with the metal-cutting machine into that cabin, and they got to work on the inner door. They wore masks, in protection against the green air which eddied out as they cut their way through. It seemed a long time to those waiting outside, but in reality it was only a matter of minutes before they were in and tackling the dazed Masters. Fritz confirmed that one of them was definitely alive, and they pulled the mask that had been prepared over his head and tightened it around his middle. I watched as they heaved him out. A cart had been drawn up beside the fallen hemisphere, and on it there was the huge crate — made of wood but sealed with a sort of tar which would keep the green air in and our own out — which was to take him. He was pulled and pushed and at last dropped in, a grotesque figure with his three short stumpy legs, long tapering conical body, three eyes and three tentacles, and that repulsive green reptilian skin I remembered with such vivid horror. The top dropped down on the crate and more men went to work at sealing it. A pipe leading from one corner was blocked temporarily; once on the boat it would be utilized to change his stale air for fresh. Then the word was given to the men on the horse teams, and the horses pulled away, dragging the cart and its cargo toward the beach.

The rest of us cleared our traces, as far as possible, from the scene. The Masters, when they came on the broken Tripod, could no longer doubt that they were facing organized opposition — it was not a casual haphazard thing such as our destruction of the Tripod on the way to the White Mountains had been — but even though this amounted to a declaration of war, there was no point in leaving unnecessary clues behind. I should have liked to do something about burying Crest, but there was no time for that. In case the trick might serve a second time, we sponged the green dye off his body and left him there. I walked apart from the others as we came away, not wanting them to see the tears that were in my eyes.

The cart was hauled out through the waves, over a firm sandy bottom, until the water lapped against the chests of the horses. The fishing boat, which had come inshore, was shallow enough in draft to get alongside, and there the crate with our prisoner was winched on board. Seeing the smoothness of the operation I was more than ever amazed and impressed by the planning that had gone into it all. The horses were unharnessed from the cart and led ashore;

from there they were scattered north and south in pairs, one ridden, one led. The rest of us heaved our wet shivering bodies over the gunwales. One thing remained to be done. A line had been fastened to the cart and, as the boat stood off, it rolled behind us till the waves closed over it. When that happened the line was cut and the boat, released from this burden, seemed to lift out of the gray waters. On shore, the horses had disappeared. All that was left was the shattered wreck of the Tripod, with a faint green mist blowing away from the mutilated hemisphere. The remaining Masters inside were certainly dead by now. What really mattered was that the jammer had worked. The Tripod lay there, crumpled and alone; there was no sign of any others coming to its help.

Our course was south. With the wind stiff and blowing only from a few points north of west, progress was slow, involving a fair amount of tacking. All available hands bent to this, and gradually the distance from our embarkation point increased. There was a headland which we needed to clear; we rounded it with painful sluggishness, wallowing in the tide, which had just begun to turn.

But now the shore was very distant, the Tripod no more than a dot on the horizon. They brought up mulled ale for us from the galley, to warm our chilled bones.

4

A Little Drink for Ruki

Julius arranged a general reshuffle once we were back at the castle. Many of those who had taken part in the capture of the Master were detailed for duties elsewhere, and Julius himself left two or three days later. The immediate crisis was over, the examination and study of our captive would take long weeks or months, and there were a dozen other strands, or more, which needed his attention and supervision. I had thought that Fritz and I might be sent away also, but this was not so. We were kept as guards. The prospect of relative inactivity was one I viewed with mixed feelings. On the one hand I could see that it might well prove boring after a time; on the other, I was not sorry to be having a rest. A long and exhausting year lay behind us.

It was also pleasant to be in fairly continuous contact with Beanpole, who was one of the examining group. Fritz and I knew each other very well by now, and got on very well, but I had missed Beanpole's more inventive and curious mind. He did not say so himself, but I knew he was viewed with a good deal of respect by the other scientists, all a great deal older than he was. He never showed the least sign of conceit over this, but he never did over anything. He was too interested in what was going to happen next to bother about himself.

In return for our various losses we had one gain, and a gain that for my part I could have well done without. This was Ulf, the erstwhile skipper of the *Erlkönig*, the barge that had been intended to take Fritz and Beanpole and me down the great river to the Games. He had been forced to leave the barge because of sickness, and Julius had appointed him as guard commander at the castle. This meant, of course, that Fritz and I were directly under his authority.

He remembered us both very well, and acted on the memories. As far as Fritz was concerned, this was all very fine. On the *Erlkönig*, as in everything else, he had obeyed orders punctiliously and without question, and been content to leave anything outside the allotted task to his superiors. Beanpole and I had been the offenders, first in persuading his assistant to let us off the barge to look for him and then, in my case, in getting myself into a brawl with the townspeople which landed me in trouble, and in Beanpole's case in disobeying him and coming to rescue me. The barge had sailed without us, and we had been forced to make our way downriver to the Games.

Beanpole did not fall under Ulf's jurisdiction, and I think Ulf was rather in awe of him, as belonging to the wise men, the scientists. My case was quite different. There was no glamour attaching to me, he was my superior officer. The fact that, despite being left behind, we had got to the Games in time, that I had won there and, with Fritz, gone on into the City and in due course come back with information, did not mollify him. If anything, it made things worse. Luck (as he saw it) was no substitute for discipline; indeed, its enemy. My example might encourage others into similar follies. Insubordination was something which needed to be borne down on, and he was the man to do the bearing down.

I recognized the bitterness but did not, at first, take it seriously. He was just, I thought, working out his resentment over my (admittedly) thoughtless behavior during our previous contact. I decided to stick it out cheerfully, and give no cause for complaint this time. Only gradually did it penetrate to me that his dislike was really deeply rooted, and that nothing I could do now was likely to change it. It was not until later that I realized how complex a man he was; nor that in attacking me he was fighting a weakness, and instability, which was part of his own nature. All I knew was that the more courteously and promptly and efficiently I obeyed instructions, the more tongue-lashings and extra duties I got. It is small wonder that within weeks I was loathing him almost as much as I had loathed my Master in the City.

His physical appearance and habits did nothing to help. His barrel-chested squatness, his thick lips and squashed nose, the mat of black hair showing through the button holes of his shirt — all these repelled me. He was the noisiest consumer of soups and stews that I had ever encountered. And his trick of continually hawking and spitting was made worse, not better, by the fact that these days he did not spit on the floor but into a red-and-white spotted handkerchief which he carried around in his sleeve. I did not know then that much of the red was his own blood, that he was a dying man. I am not sure that knowing would have made all that much difference, either. He rode me continuously, and my control of my temper wore thinner day by day.

Fritz was a great help, both in calming me down and in taking things on himself where possible. So was Beanpole, with whom I talked a lot during off-duty times. And I had another source of interest, to take my mind off things to some extent. This was our prisoner, the Master: Ruki.

He came through what must have been a harrowing and painful experience very well. The room which had been made ready for him was one of the castle dungeons, and Fritz and I attended him there, entering through an air lock and wearing face masks when we were inside. It was a big room, more then twenty feet square, much of it hewn out of solid rock. On the basis of our reports, the scientists had done everything possible to make him comfortable, even to sinking a circular hole in the floor which could be filled with warm water for him to soak in. I do not think it was, by the time we got it there in buckets, as hot as he would have liked, and it was not renewed often enough to meet the longing all the Masters had for continually soaking their lizardlike skins; but it was better than nothing. Much the same applied to the food, which had been worked out, like the air, on the basis of a few small samples Fritz had managed to bring out of the City.

Ruki was in a mild state of shock for the first couple of days, and then went into what I recognized as the Sickness, the Curse of the Skloodzi, my old Master had called it. Brown patches appeared on the green of his skin, his tentacles quivered all the time, and he himself was apathetic, not responding to stimuli. We had no way of treating him, not even the gas bubbles which the Masters in the City used to alleviate pain or discomfort, and he just had to get over it as best he could. Fortunately, he did so. I went into his cell a week after he had been taken and found him back to a healthy shade of green and showing a distinct interest in food.

Earlier, he had made no response to questions in any of the human languages we tried. He still did not do so, and we began to wonder, despondently, whether we had picked on one of the few Masters without such knowledge. After a few days of this, though, and since he was plainly back to full health, one of the scientists suspected that the ignorance was feigned, not real. We were told not to bring any hot water for his pool the next morning. He quickly showed evidence of discomfort and even indulged in sign language, going to the empty hole and waving his tentacles at it. We paid no attention to this. As we prepared to leave the room he finally spoke, in the dull booming voice they used. In German, he said, "Bring me water. I need to bathe."

I looked up at him, a wrinkled misshapen monster twice my own height.

"Say please," I told him.

But "please" was a word the Masters had never learned in any of our languages. He merely repeated, "Bring me water."

"You wait," I said. "I'll see what the scientists say."

Once the barrier was down, he did not attempt to go mute again. Nor, on the other hand, was he particularly forthcoming. He answered some questions that were put to him, and treated others with an obdurate silence. It was not always easy to work out the basis on which he chose to respond or stay silent. There were obvious blanks where questions were pertinent to a possible defense of the City, but it was difficult to see why, for instance, after talking freely on the role of human slaves and the opposition to this by some of the Masters, he should have refused to say anything about the Sphere Chase. This was the sport of which all the Masters seemed to be passionately fond, played on a triangular arena in the center of the City. I suppose in a remote way it resembled basketball, except that there were seven "baskets," the players were miniature Tripods, and the ball was a flashing golden sphere which seemed to appear out of thin air. Ruki would not answer a single question on that subject.

During my long months of slavery, I had never known the name of my Master, nor if he had a name: he was always "Master," and I was "boy." We could scarcely call our prisoner by such a title. We asked him his name, and he told us it was Ruki. In a very short time I found I was thinking of him as that — as an individual, that is, as well as a representative of the enemy, who held our world in subjection and whom we must destroy. I had known already, of course, that the Masters were not a solid mass of identical monsters. My own Master had been relatively easygoing, Fritz's brutal by comparison. They had different interests, too. But any distinctions I had made between them in the City had been severely practical; one looked for them in order to exploit them. In this altered situation, one saw things from a slightly different point of view.

One day, for instance, I had been delayed in bringing him his evening meal by something which Ulf had given me to do. I came in through the air lock to find him squatting in the center of the room, and said something about being sorry I was late. He made a slight twirling gesture with one tentacle, and boomed at me, "It is not important, when there are so many interesting things to do and to see."

The blank featureless walls of his prison were all around him, lit by the two small lamps, colored green for his convenience, which afforded illumination. The only breaks in the monotony were provided by the door and the hole in the floor. (It served as a bed for him, as well as a bath, with seaweed in place of the mossy stuff that was used in the City.) One could not read expression into these completely alien features — the neckless head with its three eyes and orifices for breathing and eating, connected by a weird pattern of wrinkles — but at this moment he looked, in a peculiar fashion, lugubrious and rueful. I realized something, at any rate: that he was making a joke! Feeble, admittedly, but a joke. It was the first indication I had had that they might have even a rudimentary sense of humor.

I had instructions to enter into conversations with him as much as possible, as Fritz did. The scientists examined him in more formal sessions, but it was thought that we might also pick something up. We reported to one of the examiners every time we left the cell, repeating what had been said word for word as far as we could. I began to find this interesting in itself, and easier. He would not always say much in reply to my promptings, but at times he did.

On the question of the slaves in the City, for

instance, he was quite voluble. It emerged that he was one of those who had opposed this. The usual basis of such opposition, as I had discovered, was not through any consideration for the poor wretches whose lives were so brutally shortened by the heat and the leaden weight, and the ill-treatment they were given, but because it was felt that dependence on slaves might weaken the strength of the Masters and eventually, perhaps, their will to survive and go on spreading their conquests through the universe. In Ruki's case, though, there seemed to be some small but genuine feeling of sympathy toward men. He did not accept that the Masters had been wrong in taking over the earth, and using the Caps to keep human beings subservient to them. He believed that men were happier in that state than they had been before the coming of the Masters. There was less disease and starvation now, and men were free of the curse of war. It was true they still resorted occasionally to violence against each other in the course of disputes, and this was horrifying enough from the Masters' point of view, but at least it was kept on that level. An end had been made to that hideous state of affairs in which men could be taken from their homes and sent to far lands, there to kill or be killed by strangers with whom they had no direct or personal quarrel. It seemed a hideous state of affairs to me, too, but I realized that Ruki's disapproval was much stronger — more passionate I would almost say — than my own.

This in itself, in his eyes, justified the conquest and the Capping. The men and women who were Capped enjoyed their lives. Even the vagrants did not appear to be particularly unhappy, and the overwhelming majority led peaceful and fruitful lives, with much ceremony and celebration.

I was reminded of a man who had been in charge of a traveling circus when I was a boy. He had talked of his animals in much the way Ruki did of men. Wild animals, he said, were subject to disease, and spent their days and nights either hunting or hunted, but in either case struggling to get enough food to avoid starvation. The ones in his circus, on the other hand, were sleek and fat. What he had said had seemed sensible then, but was not so compelling now.

Ruki, at any rate, while approving the Masters' control of the planet, and of the undisciplined warlike creatures who had previously ruled it, thought it was wrong to bring them into the City. He was confirmed in his view, of course, by finding that somehow, despite their Caps, one or more of the slaves had given information to those of us who remained in rebellion. (We had not told him that, nor anything else that could possibly be useful to the Masters, but it was not difficult for him to work out that some leakage must have occurred for us to be able to reproduce their air and food.) You could see that, despite his own captivity, he obtained a kind of satisfaction from having been proved right in his stand.

This was not to say that he had any fears that our attempts to rebel against the Masters might be successful. He seemed to be impressed by our ingenuity in having carried out the attacks against the Tripod in which he had been traveling; but it was much as a man would be impressed by a hound following a scent or a sheep dog bringing its charges back to the pen through many hazards. All this was interesting, and clever, although a nuisance to him personally. It could make no difference to the real state of things. The Masters were not to be overthrown by a handful of impudent pygmies.

He was studied in various physical ways by our scientists, apart from those sessions in which questions were asked. I was present at some. He showed no sign of resistance, or even of displeasure (though it is doubtful if we would have recognized displeasure any more than other emotions in him), but submitted to the probings and bloodlettings and staring through magnifying glasses as though these were not happening to him at all but to another. The only complaints he did make, in fact, were about the water or the room itself not being hot enough. The scientists had rigged up a form of heating by this thing called electricity, and I found the room stifling, but by his standards it was cold.

His food and drink were also tampered with. The intention was to see what effect certain substances might have on him, but the experiment did not meet with success. He seemed to have some way of sensing the presence of anything which might be harmful, and in those cases simply refused to touch what was put in front of him. On one occasion, after this had happened three times in succession, I spoke to Beanpole about it.

I asked, "Do we have to do this sort of thing? At least we were given food and water, even as slaves in the City. Ruki has been nearly two days without anything. It seems unnecessarily cruel."

Beanpole said, "It's cruel to keep him here at all, if you care to think of it that way. The cell is too small, and not warm enough, and he does not have the heavy gravity he was used to."

"Those are things that can't be helped. Putting stuff in his food and making him go without when he won't eat it is not quite the same."

"We have to do everything we can to find a weak spot in them. You found one yourself: that place between mouth and nose where a blow will kill them. But it does not help us much, because there is no way of being able to strike them all at that point at the same time. We need to find something else. Something we can use."

I saw the point, but was not entirely convinced.

"I'm sorry it has to be him. I would rather it were one of them like Fritz's Master, or even mine. Ruki does not seem so bad as most. At least, he was opposed to using men as slaves."

"So he tells you."

"But they do not lie. They cannot. I learned

that, at least, in the City. My Master could never understand the difference between story tales and lies — they were all the same to him."

"They may not lie," Beanpole said, "but they do not always tell the full truth, either. He said he was opposed to slavery. What about the plan to turn our air into the choking green gas they breathe? Has he said anything about being opposed to that?"

"He's never said anything at all about it."

"But he knows about it: they all do. He has not spoken of it because he does not know that we know. He may be not quite as bad as some of the others, but he is one of them. They have never had wars. The loyalty they have to their own kind is something which we probably do not understand any more than they can understand the way we fight among ourselves. But if we do not understand it, we must still reckon with it. And we must use every weapon we can against it. If this involves putting him to some discomfort — if it involves killing him — that is not so important. Only one thing is important: winning the struggle."

I said, "You do not need to remind me."

Beanpole smiled. "I know. Anyway, his food will be normal next time. We do not want to kill him if we can help it. There is more chance of his being useful to us if he remains alive."

"Not much sign of it so far."

"We must keep trying."

We had been sitting out on the ruined seaward battlement of the castle, enjoying an afternoon of still air and pale wintry sunshine; the sun was an orange disk dropping toward a haze-filled western horizon. The peace was interrupted now by a familiar voice, bawling from the courtyard behind us.

"Parker! Where are you, you useless lump of awkwardness? Here! And at once, I tell you."

I sighed, and prepared to stir myself. Beanpole said, "Ulf is not getting too much for you, I hope, Will."

I shrugged. "It would be all the same, if he were."

He said, "We want you and Fritz as Ruki's attendants because you are both used to them, and so are better at noticing anything strange and reporting it. But I do not think Julius realized how much friction there would be between you and Ulf."

"The friction you get," I said, "between a log of wood and a saw. And I am not the saw."

"If it is too difficult . . . it would be possible for you to be transferred to other duties."

He said it diffidently, as much as anything else, I think, because he did not wish to emphasize his own higher status — that he could in fact arrange something like this.

I said, "I can put up with him."

"Perhaps if you did not make such a point of doing just that . . ."

"Doing what?"

"Putting up with him. I think it makes him angrier."

I was astonished. I said, with some indignation, "I obey orders, and promptly. What more can he ask?"

Beanpole sighed. "Yes. Well, I'd better be getting back to work myself, anyway."

I had noticed one difference between Ulf of the *Erlkönig* and the one who now made my life a misery at the castle. The old Ulf had been a drinking man: the whole business of Beanpole and me leaving the barge had started when he did not return on time and his assistant suspected that he had gone drinking in one of the town's taverns. Here he did not drink at all. Some of the older men would take an occasional nip of brandy, against the cold as they said, but not he. He did not even drink the beer, which was a more common drink, or the rough red wine that was served with our dinner. At times I wished that he would. I felt it might help to sweeten his temper a little.

Then one day a messenger from Julius came to the castle. I have no idea what message he brought, but he also carried with him a couple of long brown stone jars. And it seemed that he was an old acquaintance of Ulf's. The jars contained schnapps, a raw colorless spirit which was drunk in Germany and which, it seemed, he and Ulf had often drunk together. Perhaps it was the unexpected sight of an old friend which weakened Ulf's resolution, or perhaps it was just that he preferred schnapps to the drinks that had been available in the castle. At any rate, I noticed the two of them sitting together in the guard-room, a jar between them and a small tumbler in front of each. I was glad to have Ulf distracted by anything, and happily kept out of the way.

In the afternoon, the messenger went on again, but he left the remaining jar with Ulf. Ulf was already showing signs of intoxication — he had not bothered to eat anything at midday — and he broached the second jar and sat drinking on his own. He appeared to have settled into a melancholy mood, not talking to anyone and seemingly not noticing much of what was going on around him. This was, of course, very wrong in a guard commander, though it might be said in his defense that the only conceivable danger to the castle were the Tripods and that things anyway had settled into a routine in which we all knew our duties and carried them out. For my part, I was not concerned either with censuring or finding justification for him, but simply glad of the absence of his raucous voice.

It had been a dark day, and light left the sky early. I prepared Ruki's meal — a porridgelike mess, more liquid than solid, from ingredients supplied by the scientists — and crossed the guardroom with it on my way to the corridor leading to his cell. The natural light in the guard-room came from a couple of windows, high up and now shaded by dusk. I could only just make out the figure of Ulf, behind his table, with the jar in front of him. I ignored him, but he called to me, "Where d'you think you're going?"

His voice was slurred a little. I said, "Taking the prisoner his meal, sir."

"Come here!"

I went and stood in front of the table, holding the tray. Ulf said, "Why haven't you lit the lamp?"

"It's not time yet."

Nor was it. It wanted another quarter hour to the time laid down by Ulf himself. If I had lit it early, on account of the day's early darkening, he would have been as likely to pick on that as a breach of one of his rules.

"Light it," he said. "And don't answer me back, Parker. When I tell you to do something, you do it, and do it fast. Is that understood?"

"Yes, sir. But the regulations say . . ."

He stood up, swaying slightly, from his seat, and leaned forward with his hands on the table. I could smell the spirits on his breath.

"You're insub . . . insubordinate, Parker, and I won't stand for it. You'll take an extra duty tonight. And now you'll put that tray down, and light the lamp. Is that clear?"

I did as I was told, silently. The lamplight gleamed on his heavy face, flushed with drink. I said coldly, "If that is all, sir, I will proceed with my duties."

He stared at me a moment. "Can't wait to get in to that pal of yours, is that it? Chatting with the big lizard is easier than working — that right?"

I moved to pick up the tray. "May I go now, sir?"

"Wait."

I stood there obediently. Ulf laughed, picked up the tumbler, and emptied it into the bowl of food prepared for Ruki. I looked at it without moving.

"Go on," he said. "Take your pal his supper. Got a little something in it to liven him up now."

I knew perfectly well what I ought to have done. Ulf was indulging in a silly drunken jest. I should have taken the tray out and made up another bowl for Ruki, throwing this one away. Instead, I asked, in the most obedient but contemptuous fashion, "Is that an order, sir?"

His anger was as great as mine, but hot where mine was cold. And his mind was blurred by drink. He said, "Do as you're told, Parker. And jump to it!"

I picked up the tray and left. I had a glimpse of what Beanpole had meant — I could have mollified Ulf with a little effort, and passed the whole thing off. I am afraid that what I was thinking was that this time he had put himself in the wrong. Ruki would refuse the food, as he refused anything which differed even slightly from what he was used to. I would have to report on this, and the incident would then be brought to light. Simply by obeying orders and acting according to regulations, I had my chance to get my own back at my tormentor.

As I reached the air lock, I heard Ulf bellowing

something in the distance. I went through into the cell, and put the tray down. I left it there, and went back to see what the yelling was about. Ulf was standing unsteadily on his feet. He said, "Belay that order. Make another supper up for the lizard."

I said, "I've taken the tray in, sir. As instructed."

"Then bring it out again! Wait. I'm coming with you."

I was annoyed that my scheme had misfired. Ruki would eat the substitute meal, and so there would be nothing that I would be obliged to report. Reporting Ulf simply for being drunk on duty was not a thought that appealed to me even in my present state of resentment. I went with him in silence, bitterly conscious of the fact that he was going to get away with it, after all.

There was barely room for two in the air lock. We were forced to jostle against each other, putting on the face masks which we must wear inside the cell. Ulf opened the inner door, and stepped through first. I heard him give a grunt of surprise and dismay. He moved forward quickly, and I could see what he had seen.

The bowl was empty. And Ruki was stretched out, full length and motionless.

Julius came back to the castle for the conference. He seemed to be limping worse than ever, but was no less cheerful and confident. He sat at the center of the long table, with the scientists, including Beanpole, clustered around him. Fritz and I sat inconspicuously at the end. André, the commander of the castle, addressed the meeting first. He said, "Our best plan always was to sabotage the Cities from within. The question was: how? We can get a certain number inside, but nowhere near enough to fight the Masters, on their own ground especially. We could wreck some of their machines, perhaps, but that would not amount to destroying the City as such. They could almost certainly repair them, and we would be worse off than before — because then they would be warned, and ready for any attack we tried to launch. This same applies to any attempt to damage the Wall. Even if we were able to cut through, which is doubtful, we could not do it on a large enough scale — either from outside or within — to prevent the Masters hitting back, and making good the damage.

"What has been needed was a way of hitting at the Masters themselves, all of them and at the same time. One suggestion was to poison their air. It might be possible, but I don't see a chance of our developing anything in the time available. Water offered a better opportunity. They use water a lot, for drinking as well as bathing. Even allowing for the fact that they are twice the height and four times the weight, they have a liquid intake four to six times that of the average man. If we could get something into their water supplies, it might do the trick.

"Unfortunately, as we have established with

the prisoner, they are sensitive to adulterants. This one simply refused anything which might harm him. Until, by a lucky chance, some schnapps was poured into his food. He consumed the food without hesitation, and was paralyzed in less than a minute."

Julius asked, "How long did it take him to recover from the paralysis?"

"He began to show signs of consciousness after about six hours. He was fully conscious after twelve, but still lacking in coordination and fairly obviously confused. Within twenty-four hours, recovery was complete."

"And since then?"

"Apparently normal," André said. "Mark you, he's still worried, and alarmed, by what happened. Not quite so confident as he was about the hopelessness of our efforts, I think."

Julius said, "How do you account for it? The paralysis?"

André shrugged. "We know that with men alcohol interferes with that part of the mind that controls the working of the body. A drunken man cannot walk straight or use his hands properly. He may even fall over. If he has taken enough, then he becomes paralyzed, as Ruki did. It seems that, in this respect, they are more sensitive and more vulnerable than we are. Equally important, the discrimination against harmful substances doesn't work in this case. The amount of alcohol apparently can be quite small. There were only the dregs of a glass in this case.

It gives us a chance, I think."

"Alcohol in their drinking water," Julius said. "Not from outside, presumably. We know that they have a purifying and treatment machine inside the Wall. From inside, then. If we can get a team in. But how about the alcohol? Even though the amount needed is small per individual, it amounts to a very large quantity altogether. You could not get that inside."

"Our men could produce it there," André said. "There are sugars in the City: they use them in making both their own foods and the food of the slaves. All that is needed is to set up distillation equipment. Then, when there is enough, introduce it to the drinking water."

Someone said, in a tone of excitement, "It might work!"

André's eyes were on Julius. He said, "It would have to be done in all three Cities simultaneously. They know that they have some opposition — our destroying the Tripod and making off with one of their number will have told them that. But the latest reports tell us they are still taking human slaves into the City, which means they still trust those they have Capped. Once they find we can pose as Capped, things will be very different."

Julius nodded slowly. "We must strike while they are unsuspecting," he said. "It is a good plan. Go ahead with preparations."

I was called later to see Julius. He was writing

in a book, but looked up as I entered the room.

"Ah, Will," he said. "Come and sit down. You know Ulf has gone?"

"I saw him leave this morning, sir."

"With some satisfaction, I gather?" I did not answer. "He is a very sick man, and I have sent him south to the sun. He will serve us there, as he has done all his life, for the short time that remains to him. He is also a very unhappy man. Even though things turned out well, he sees only failure: his failure to conquer an old weakness. Do not despise him, Will."

"No, sir."

"You have your own weaknesses. They are not his, but they lead you into folly. As they did this time. Ulf's folly lay in getting drunk, yours in putting pride before sense. Shall I tell you something? I brought Ulf and you together again partly because I thought it would do you good — teach you to accept discipline and so to think more carefully before you acted. It does not seem to have had the result that I hoped for."

I said, "I'm sorry, sir."

"Well, that's something. So is Ulf. He told me something, before he left. He blamed himself for you and Beanpole going astray at your first encounter. He knew he ought not to have stayed in the town, and thus given you the excuse to go ashore looking for him. If I had known this, I would not have let him come here. Some people are oil and water. It seems that you and he were."

He was silent for a moment or two, but I felt more uncomfortable than ever under the scrutiny of his deep-set blue eyes. He said, "This expedition that is being planned. Do you wish to take part in it?"

I said, quickly and with conviction, "Yes, sir!"

"My rational impulse is to refuse your request. You have done well, but you have not learned to master your rashness. I am not sure that you ever will."

"Things have turned out well, sir. As you said."

"Yes, because you have been lucky. So I am going to be irrational, and send you. And it is also true that you know the City, and will be valuable for that reason. But I think, to be honest, it is your luck that makes the biggest impression on me. You are a kind of mascot to us, Will."

Fervently, I said, "I will do my best, sir."

"Yes, I know. You can go now."

I had reached the door when he called me back.

"One thing, Will."

"Yes, sir?"

"Spare a thought now and then for those who do not have luck on their side. For Ulf, in particular."

5

Six Against the City

It was in spring, not of the next year but the year after, that the expedition was launched.

In between there had been so many things to do and to prepare, plans to be made, equipment to be fashioned, actions to be rehearsed again and again. Contacts had to be made, also, with those who had gone out to form centers of resistance in the region of the other two Cities. Things would have been easier if we had been able to use the means of sending messages through the air on invisible rays, which our forefathers had used and which the Masters used themselves. Our scientists could have built machines for this, but the decision went against it. The Masters must be kept in their state of false security. If we used the thing called radio, they would detect it, and whether or not they tracked down our transmitters, they would know that a large-scale rebellion was afoot.

So we were forced to rely on the primitive means we had. We spread a network of carrier pigeons, and for the rest relied on fast horses and hard riding, using both riders and horses in relays as much as possible. Plans were coordinated far in advance, and men from the distant centers returned for briefings on them.

One of those who returned was Henry. I did not recognize him easily; he had grown, and thinned, and was bronzed with long exposure to the hot sun of the tropics. He was very confident, and pleased with the way things had gone. They had found a resistance movement rather like our own, to the north of the isthmus on which the second City of the Masters stood, and had joined forces with it. The interchange of information had been useful, and he had brought one of the leaders back with him. He was a tall, lank, sunburned man called Walt, who spoke little and in an odd twangy voice when he did so.

We talked through an afternoon — Henry and I and Beanpole — of times past and times to come. In between talking, we watched a demonstration arranged by the scientists. This was late summer, and we looked from the castle wall across a sea calm and blue, barely wrinkled out to the far horizon. It was all very peaceful, a world in which one could imagine there were no such things as Tripods or Masters. (The Tripods never did come near this isolated stretch of coast, in fact. That was one of the reasons the castle had been chosen.) Directly beneath us, a small group clustered around two figures dressed in shorts, such as those I had worn as a slave in the City. The resemblance did not end there, because they also wore, over head and shoulders, a mask similar to the one that had protected me against the poisonous air of the

Masters. With one difference: where the pouch with filter had been there was a tube, and the tube ran to a boxlike thing strapped to the back.

A signal was given. The two figures moved across the rocks and waded into the water. It rose to cover their knees, their thighs, their chests. Then, together, they plunged forward and disappeared below the surface. For a second or two one could see them dimly, shadowy figures striking out, away from the castle. After that, they were lost, and we watched and waited for them to reappear.

It was a long wait. Seconds became minutes. Although I had been told what to expect, I grew apprehensive. I was sure that something had gone wrong, that they had drowned in that limitless azure serenity. They had been swimming against the tide, which was coming in from the ocean. There were strange undercurrents in these parts, and submerged reefs. Time passed, slowly but relentlessly.

The object of all this was to help us get into the Cities. We could not use the method we had used previously; something more direct and more certain had to be found. The obvious solution was to reverse the process by which Fritz and I had escaped, and get in from the river, through the discharge vents. All three Cities stood on watercourses, so the method would apply universally. The difficulty was that, even going with the flow of water, the passage had taxed our physical resources to their limit and, in my case, beyond. To swim up against the tide would be quite impossible without aid.

I burst out at last, "It hasn't worked! They can't be still alive down there."

Beanpole said, "Wait."

"It must have been over ten minutes . . ."

"Nearer fifteen."

Henry said suddenly, "Over there. Look!"

I looked where he was pointing. Far out on the glassy blue, a dot had appeared, followed by another. Two heads. Henry said, "It worked, but I don't understand how."

Beanpole did his best to explain to us. It was something to do with the air, which I had always thought of as a sort of invisible nothing, being made up of two different nothings, two gases, and the part that was smaller being the part we needed to keep alive. The scientists had learned how to separate the two, and keep the useful part in those containers on the swimmers' backs. Things called valves regulated a supply of it to the masks the men wore. One could stay submerged for a long time. Flippers attached to the feet would enable one to swim strongly against a tide. We had found our means of entering the Cities.

The next morning, Henry left. He took the lean taciturn stranger with him. He also took a supply of the masks, and the tubes and boxes that went with them.

From a dugout by the river bank, I looked at the City of Gold and Lead again, and could not entirely repress the tremor that ran through my body. The ramparts of gold, topped with the emerald bubble of its protective dome, stretched across the river and the land on either side, immense and massive and seemingly impregnable. It was ludicrous to imagine that it could be overthrown by the half dozen of us who had collected here.

None of the Capped would venture so close to the City, having such an awe of it, so we were safe from any interference by them. We saw Tripods in plenty, of course, giant-striding across the sky on journeys to or from the City, but we were not near any of the routes they used. We had been here three days, and this was the last. As daylight faded from a blustery gray sky, it took with it the last few hours before the moment of decision.

It had not been easy to synchronize the attacks on the three Cities. The actual entries had to be made at different times, because the cover of darkness varied throughout the world. The one in which Henry was concerned would follow six hours after ours. That in the east was taking place just about now, in the middle of the night. That City, we all knew, represented the riskiest part of the enterprise. Our base out there was the smallest and weakest of the three, existing in a land where the Capped were entirely alien and spoke an incomprehensible language. Our recruits had been few. Those who were to make the attack had come to the castle the previous autumn; they were slim, yellow-skinned boys who spoke little and smiled less. They had learned a little German, and Fritz and I had briefed them on what they would find inside the City (we presumed that all three Cities would be much the same), and they had listened and nodded, but we had not been sure how much they understood.

At any rate, there was nothing we could do about that now. We had to concentrate on our job here. Darkness gathered, over the City, the river, the surrounding plain, and the distant hump that was the ruin of a great-city of old. We had our last meal of ordinary human food in the open air. After this, it would be a matter of relying on what we could find in the City — eating the slaves' tasteless food in the protection of one of the refuge rooms.

I looked at my companions in the last light. They were dressed as the slaves were, and had the masks ready to put on, and their skins, like my own, had been rendered pale by a winter spent completely under cover from the sun. We wore the false-Caps closely fitted to our skulls, our hair growing through them. But they did not look like slaves, and I wondered how the deception could succeed. Surely the first Master who saw one of us would realize the truth, and raise the alarm?

But the time had passed for doubts and brooding. A star gleamed in the sky, not far above the western horizon. Fritz, the leader of our troop, looked at the watch which he alone carried and which he must keep hidden in the belt of his shorts. It kept perfect time and would work even underwater, and had been made not by our own scientists but by the great craftsmen who lived before the time of the Masters. It reminded me of the one I had found in the ruins of the first great-city, and lost when boating on the river with Eloise, at the Château de la Tour Rouge — how far away all that seemed now!

"It is time," Fritz said. "In we go."

Spies before us had traced the underwater configuration of the vents through which we had to swim. They were large, fortunately, and there were four of them, each presumably leading back to a pool like the one into which we had plunged. They came out twenty feet below the surface of the water. One by one, we dived and forced our way against the current, guided by small lights fixed on bands about our foreheads: another wonder of the ancients, but this time recreated by Beanpole and his colleagues. Beanpole had had to stay back at headquarters, despite his pleas to come with us. It was not just that he was too valuable to be spared. There was also the weakness of his eyes. Spectacles would not work underwater, and would also set him unmistakably apart from the other slaves in the City.

The lights moved in front of me, and I saw one wink out. That must be the vent. I swam farther down and saw a curved edge of metal, and the shadowy outline of a tunnel wall. I kicked my flippered legs and went forward.

The tunnel seemed interminable. There was the flicker of the light ahead of me, the dim swath of my own lamp, and always the pressure of water against which I must force my body. There was a time when I wondered if we were getting anywhere at all — was it possible that the current was so strong that our seeming to move against it was an illusion? That we were doing no more than hold our own, and would stay suspended here in this featureless tube of a world until tiredness overcame us and we were pushed back to the outlet in the river? The water seemed to have gotten a little warmer, but that could be another illusion. At that moment, though, the light in front disappeared, and I forced my weary limbs to a greater effort. From time to time, I had touched the roof of the tunnel with my outstretched hand. I tried again, and found nothing solid. And above, far above, there was a glimmer of green.

I swam up, and at last my head broke water. By prearrangement, we made for the side, where we would be hidden by the wall around the pool. The one who had been in front of me was there, too, treading water: we nodded in silence. Other heads bobbed up, one by one, and with immense relief I saw Fritz.

The last time, the pool had been deserted by night, but we could take no chances. Fritz cautiously heaved himself up the side, and peered over. He waved to the rest of us, and we climbed out, onto solid ground. And into the crushing leaden weight of the City's gravity. I saw my companions, prewarned but shaken for all that, stagger under the sudden strain. Their shoulders sagged. The spring had gone out of their limbs, as I knew it had gone out of my own. I realized that we might not look so very different from the slaves, after all.

Quickly, we did what was necessary, unclipping the tubes from our masks and unstrapping the oxygen tanks from our backs. This left us with ordinary masks, with sponge filters in the neck pouches which we would renew later in one of the communal places that the slaves used. We punctured the tanks and lashed them and the tubes together. Then one of us climbed back into the pool for a moment, and held them under till they filled. They sank down. The current would take them out into the river. Even if one of the Capped fished them out, tomorrow or the day after, he would make nothing of them. He would take them for another of the mysteries of the Tripods; as we knew, solid debris did emerge from the City from time to time.

We could talk to each other, but were anxious to make no unnecessary noise. Fritz nodded again, and we set off. Past the nets which took heat out of the water, so that beyond the last one the surface steamed and even bubbled in places, past the great cascade that formed the pool, along by stacks of crates reaching up to the pointed roof of the hall, and so to the steep curving ramp which marked the way out. The light around us was a dim green, from the globes which hung from the ceiling. Fritz led the way, advancing warily from cover to cover, and we followed at his signal. Few of the Masters were active at night, but it would not do to be surprised by one; because no slave would be abroad. Moreover, we were carrying certain things we had brought with us, parts of the distillation apparatus which we might not be able to find here.

Slowly and carefully we made our way across the sleeping City. We passed places where there was the hum of busy machinery, and we passed the deserted garden pools in which ugly, somber-colored plants looked like menacing sentient beings themselves. We made our cautious way along one side of the great arena on which the Sphere Chase was played. Looking at these, and other familiar places, the days, years of the free life I had known seemed to disappear. I could almost think that I was on my way back to that apartment in 19 Pyramid where my Master would be waiting for me. Waiting for me to make his bed, rub his back, prepare his meal — or even just to talk to him, to give him the companionship which, in some strange non-Masterlike way, he wanted.

It was a long journey, made more protracted by our determination to run no risk. By the time we reached the area we sought, the area, on the opposite side of the City, where the river came in, to be purified and treated for the Masters, the darkness overhead was beginning to turn green. In the world outside, a clean dawn would be breaking over the distant hills. We were tired and hot, clammy with our own sweat, thirsty and aching under the never-ending strain of the weight that dragged us down. Many hours must elapse still before we would be able to slip into one of the refuges, remove our masks, and eat and drink. I wondered how the four who were new to all this were taking it. At least Fritz and I had been through it before.

We were crossing an open triangular space, keeping under the cover of gnarled treelike plants that leaned out of the inevitable pool. Fritz went on a stage, stopped, and waved for others to follow. I, as rear guard, would be the last to go. As I prepared, I saw, instead of a beckoning wave, his hand held up in warning. I froze to my spot, and waited. There was a sound in the distance: a series of rhythmic slapping noises. I knew what that was. Three feet coming down in succession on the smooth stone.

A Master. My skin prickled as I saw him, in the dim green twilight, passing along the far side of the plaza. I thought that, having seen so much of Ruki over so long a time, I had grown used to them, but Ruki had been our prisoner, confined to that small featureless room. Looking at this one, at large in the City which was the symbol of their power and dominance, all the old fear returned, and the old hatred.

Fritz and I had found, during our sojourn here, that there were many places in the City which were rarely if ever used. A lot of these were storehouses of some kind, stacked with crates, like the cavern through which we had entered, or empty in preparation for some future use. I imagine that in building the City, they had allowed space for expansion, and that a lot of it had not yet been taken up.

At any rate, this was something of which we could take advantage. The Masters, as exemplified in the unvarying routes so often followed by the Tripods, were creatures of repetitious habit in many ways; and the human slaves would never venture anywhere except on a direct errand. It would have been unthinkable for them to pry into what they regarded as the holy mysteries of the gods.

We headed for a pyramid which Fritz had previously explored, and which was less than a hundred yards from the ramp leading down to the water purification plant. It was obvious that the ground floor was not in use; a brownish fuzz, slowly growing and easily brushed off by contact, covered the exposed surfaces of the crates. (There were a number of such funguslike growths in the City, which the Masters did not seem to bother about.) To make ourselves doubly safe, though, we went down the spiral ramp to the basement, where the crates were stacked even higher. We cleared a space at the far corner, and began at once to set up our apparatus.

We were depending on the resources of the City itself for a good part of our equipment. Glass tubes, for instance, and jars, we knew to be available. What we had brought with us were chiefly small tools, and rubber tubes and sealers. Another item for which we were going to poach on our enemy was the form of heating. There were no open fires here, but there were devices which no longer seemed as magical as they once had. These were pads, of various sizes, which, when a button was pressed, gave off a concentrated radiant heat: the smaller ones were used by the slaves to heat liquids to boiling point for their Masters. The pads had attachments which fitted into sockets in the walls of the buildings, and when heat stopped being produced they were fitted in and left for an hour or so, after which they were as good as new. Beanpole had explained that it must be a form of the same electricity which our scientists had rediscovered.

Day broke, the light paled through different shades of green, and there was even a pale, barely visible disk which was the sun. In two shifts, Fritz guiding one and I the other, we went to one of the communal places, to freshen ourselves, to eat and drink and replace the filters which we used in our masks. This, too, had been carefully chosen. It was the communal place attached to one of the major pyramids, where a large number of Masters, from different parts of the City, met daily to conduct some sort of business. (Like so many other things, the business itself was quite baffling.) This meant that there was a large and constant turnover of slaves who had accompanied their Masters and whose services had been dispensed with for the time being. Some, Fritz had noted, were there for hours, sleeping on the couches, and the majority of them did not know each other except as vague characterless figures, with whom they jostled for places at the dispensing machines or for vacant couches. All the slaves, of course, were always so exhausted that they had little energy for observation, anyway.

This was to be our principal supply base, not only as far as food and water were concerned, but for the equally pressing needs of recuperation and sleep. We had decided that we must work by night, and snatch what rest we could during the day. This could not be much — a few hours at a time.

During the first day, we foraged for the things we needed. It was astonishing how smoothly it went. André had been right in saying that the three attacks had to be made simultaneously, because the whole hope of our success depended on the absolute confidence the Masters had in their control of Capped humans. We could go where we liked and take what we liked, because it was unthinkable that we should be doing anything that was not directed by them. We labored through the streets with our booty right under the noses of the enemy. Two of us dragged a vat, on a small wheeled trailer, through an open space in which, on either side, a dozen or more Masters disported with solemn lack of grace in steaming water.

The vats were our initial and primary requisition. We got three of them down into our basement and filled them with a mash made of water and the biscuitlike food which was available to slaves in the communal places. The resultant evil-looking concoction was a starchy mess to which we added a little of the dried yeast which we had brought with us. It was not long before it was fermenting — the scientists had said this would happen, even in the different air of the City, but it was a relief to see the bubbles forming, all the same. The first stage was under way.

As soon as we had got it started, we began constructing the distillation unit which would perform the necessary concentrating function. This was not so easy. The normal distillation process involves heating a liquid so that it forms steam. Alcohol, which is what we were hoping to produce, boils at a lower temperature than water, and so the first steam that was given off would have a lot of alcohol in it. The next step should be to cool the steam, so that it condenses back into a liquid. Repeating this process produces progressively more and more concentrated alcohol.

Unfortunately, we faced the problem of the unchanging and all-pervading heat here. We had hoped to overcome it by running longer lengths of tubing, giving the steam more time to cool, but it was soon apparent that this was not going to work. The amount trickling through was pitiful — a slow drip which looked as though it would take months to fill the collecting jar. We had to find another way of handling it.

That night, Fritz and I went out together. We traveled cautiously down the ramp to the cavern which held the water purification plant. The green lights were on, and the machines throbbed with power, but there was no one there. The machines worked automatically, and what need was there to set a guard in a place where the only living things were the Masters and their blindly obedient slaves? (Not a single door anywhere in the City had a lock on it.) On this side of the machines, a pool of seething hot water, more than twenty feet across, drained into a number of different vents which took it on its multifarious courses — to be pumped up to the top floors of the pyramids, or to form the supply for many garden pools and similar amenities at ground level. But beyond . . .

There was another pool here, feeding into the machines. In turn, it was fed from a wide arched tunnel, set in the dull seamless gold of the Wall. We climbed a retaining wall, and found ourselves standing on a narrow ledge, which ran back into the tunnel. We went along it, into increasing darkness.

Coolness struck up to us from the tumbling surface of the water. This was what we were looking for, what we must have. But we needed more space than the ledge offered if we were to set up a distillation apparatus here. Fritz was ahead of me. I could no longer make him out, and only knew he had stopped when the sound of footfalls ceased. I called softly, "Where are you?"

"Here. Take my hand."

We were right under the Wall by now. The water had a different noise to it, more riotous, and I guessed this must be the point where it bubbled free of its underground confinement. It must come in from the outer world at a depth low enough to make sure that no air came with it. Groping after Fritz, I found myself moving out over the area which earlier had been occupied by the river. There was a kind of platform, stretching across the tunnel, and leading to a smaller tunnel which continued outward, directly above the now hidden and subterranean stream. We found what appeared to be the manhole cover for an inspection chamber, and presumably there were others. I imagine they were there against the possibility of a blockage. They would have had to use the Capped for checking, if so — none of the Masters could have got into so confined a space.

Fritz said, "There is room, Will."

I objected, "It's pitch black."

"We will have to manage. And the eyes become accustomed. I can see a little better already, I think."

I could scarcely see anything. But he was right — we should have to manage. It was the coolant we needed, and here it was, swirling below us in abundance.

I asked, "Can we start tonight?"

"We can get some of the stuff along, at least."

In the nights that followed, we worked frantically to build up supplies. There was a plentiful supply of containers, made of a stuff like glass but yet yielding a little to the touch, and we filled these with the product of our labors. There would not have been room for them on the platform, but we were able to stack them along the narrower tunnel. I prayed that there would be no underground blockage in the river, calling for inspection, during this time. It did not seem likely that there would. The system was obviously designed for an emergency, and had probably never been used since the City was built.

It was an exhausting life. In the tunnel, one had some escape from the heat, but the gravity still pulled one down and there was still the need to wear the irritating face masks. We were badly short of sleep, also. There were only about twelve hours a day during which it was practicable to use the communal rooms, and we had to take our rest there in shifts. It could be frustrating when the place was full of slaves. On one occasion, dog-tired, I got there to find every couch occupied. I dropped and slept on the hard floor until I was awakened by a hand on my shoulder, and realized, with aching eyes and protesting limbs, that I must get up again, put on my mask, and go out into the green mist that was our nearest approach to daylight.

But time passed, and slowly our supplies built up. We were working to a schedule and a program, and met our target with nearly a week to spare. We went on making alcohol. It was better than simply marking time and waiting, and the higher the concentration we managed to get into the Masters' water supply, presumably the more effective it was likely to be. We had already traced which of the conduits leading from the inner pool supplied the drinking water system. We were ready for the day, and the hour, that had been arranged. At last it came.

It offered, as far as we here were concerned, one snag. We had no idea how soon the effects would start showing in the Masters, nor at what stage they would begin to realize that something was wrong. The three Cities, we knew, were in communication with each other, and it would not do for one to alert the others to a possible danger. So the drinking water in each had to be tampered with at roughly the same time.

And there, of course, we faced the problem set by the fact that our world was a globe, revolving around the sun. The water purification plants had a daytime staff of Masters, who looked after the machines on three separate shifts, but were unattended at night. It had been realized that two out of the three attempts could be made in this interval; one just after the day's work ended, the other not long before it began. That left the third City not far from midday when the sabotage attempt must be made.

It had been agreed without question that ours was the expedition which must tackle this problem. We had the advantage of being closer to headquarters and also of having in our number two who knew the inside of the City by experience. It was up to us somehow to complete our task while Masters were actually on duty at the plant. The alternative was to run the risk of finding our enemies alerted and ready to fight back.

We gave a lot of thought to this. Although we had got away with carting pieces of equipment around, and the four newcomers had grown so used to the presence of the Masters as to be almost contemptuous of them — this did not happen with Fritz or me, whose memories were still bitter — it was extremely unlikely that they would fail to question it if they saw us carrying containers out from the tunnel and emptying them into one of the conduits. This was, after all, their own department, and any humans working there would be under their orders.

One of us suggested posing as a slave who had a message, calling them away to some other part of the City. Since they never mistrusted the slaves, they would not doubt the genuineness of it. Fritz dismissed the idea.

"It would be a strange message, and they might think the slave confused. They would be likely to check with other Masters, perhaps in the place to which they were told to go. Remember that they can talk to each other at long distances. In any case, I am sure that they would not all go. One at least would stay at the machines."

"Then what?"

"There is only one possibility, really." We looked at him, and I nodded. "We must use force."

The maximum number of Masters on duty at any particular time was four, but one only appeared occasionally; I think he was a supervisor of some kind. Usually there were three of them, but one of these would frequently be absent, taking a dip in a nearby garden pool. Even armed with the knowledge of that vulnerable spot between nose and mouth, and with six of us, we could not hope to deal with more than two. Under equal conditions they would have been so much bigger and stronger than we were; here, under their gravity, the contest would have been quite hopeless. We had no weapons, and no means of making any.

The moment we had chosen was roughly halfway through the middle shift of the day. It was necessary to be ready to act as soon as the third Master came up the ramp and headed for the garden pool, which meant that we had to have cover within easy reach and observation of the entrance to the plant. Fritz solved the problem by getting us to cut branches from trees in the pool during the night and pile them in a heap: this was frequently done by way of pruning, and the branches left until a squad of slaves came to remove them. We could bank on their going unnoticed for a day, at least. So, having been in turn to the communal place, we surreptitiously snuggled into the pile, which had something of the texture of seaweed — a clinging rubbery loathsomeness, seeming almost alive. Fritz was in a position where he could look out, the rest of us deeply buried and running, I thought, some risk of smothering if things were too long delayed.

The delay appeared to be very long indeed. I lay in this unpleasant nest, with nothing to see but the fronds in front of my face, dying to know what was happening outside but not daring even to whisper a question. The stuff was getting sticky, too, probably because it was decaying already, which did not make the wait any more attractive. I found I had a cramp in one leg, but could not move to ease it. The pain got worse, and I did not see how I could bear it much longer. I would have to get up, massage it . . .

"Now," Fritz said.

There was no one about. We raced for the ramp, or, at least, lumbered a little faster than usual. At the bottom, we slowed. One Master was in view, the other out of sight behind one of the machines. As we approached, he said, "What is it? You have some errand here?"

"A message, Master. It is . . ."

Three of us, simultaneously, grabbed for tentacles. Fritz leaped and the other two braced his legs as high as they could. It was over almost at once. Fritz struck hard at the weak spot and with a single ear-splitting howl, the Master collapsed, throwing us away as he did so.

We had thought the second one would be more of a problem, but in fact he was easier to cope with. He came around from behind the machine, saw us standing by his fallen colleague, and asked, "What happened here?"

We made the ritual bow of reverence. Fritz said, "The Master is hurt, Master. We do not know how."

Once more their absolute confidence in the devotion of their slaves gave us the chance we needed. Without hesitation or suspicion, he came forward and bent down slightly, probing at the other with his tentacles. That brought the openings which were his nose and mouth within reach of Fritz's fist without his having to jump. This one dropped without even crying out.

"Drag them out of sight behind the machine," Fritz ordered. "Then get on with the work."

No urging was necessary. We had about half an hour before the third Master came back. Two worked in the tunnel, bringing the containers out along the narrow ledge; the rest of us carried them, two at a time, from there to the drinking water conduit, and tipped them in. There were about a hundred containers altogether. A dozen trips should do it. The colorless liquid splashed into the water, mixing with it and disappearing. I ticked off my staggering runs. Nine . . . ten . . . eleven . . .

The tentacle caught me without my even seeing it. The Master must have come to the top of the ramp and for some reason paused to look down, instead of proceeding with the usual slap of feet, which we would have heard. It was the supervisor, we realized later, making one of his periodic visits. He obviously saw the procession of slaves with containers, saw the contents being tipped into the conduit, and was curious. He came down, spinning — which was their equivalent of running and which was almost silent because only the point of one foot made intermittent contact with the ground. His tentacle tightened around my waist.

"Boy," he demanded, "what is this? Where are the Masters?"

Mario, who had been directly behind me, dropped his container and jumped. He was gripped by the second tentacle in midair. The one that held me bit in, squeezing breath from my body. I saw the other two coming up, but could do nothing. I heard myself scream as the squeezing became unbearable. With his third tentacle, the Master flailed at the Dutch boy, Jan, tossing him, as though he were a doll, against the nearest machine. He then picked up Carlos with it. The three of us were as helpless as trussed chickens.

He did not know of the two in the tunnel, but that was small consolation. They would be bound to check the water. We had come so close to success, and now . . .

Jan was getting painfully to his feet. I was upside down, my masked head brushing against the lower part of the Master's body. I saw Jan get a hand on something, a bolt of metal, about six inches long and a couple of inches thick, which was used in some way for adjusting one of the machines. And I remembered — before he was switched to this expedition he had been preparing for a possible entry in the Games . . . as a discus-thrower. But if the Master saw him . . . I reached down with my hands, and wrenched at the nearest stubby leg, trying to dig my nails in.

It had as little effect as a gnat biting a cart horse. He must have been aware of it, though, because the tentacle tightened again. I yelled in pain. The agony increased. I was on the point of blacking out. I saw Jan twist his body, tense it for the throw. Then came oblivion.

I recovered, to find myself propped against one of the machines. Rather than try to revive me, the others had, rightly, got on with the job. I was bruised and when I drew breath it was like inhaling fire. The Master lay not far from me on the floor, oozing a greenish ichor from a gash

gash just below the mouth. I watched, dazed, as the last of the containers was tipped. Fritz came up, and said, "Get all the empty containers back to the tunnel, in case another of them comes." He saw that I was conscious. "How are you feeling, Will?"

"Not so bad. Have we really done it?"

He looked at me, and a rare grin spread over his long solemn face.

"I think we have. I really think we have."

We crept quietly up the ramp, and away. Out in the open, a Master saw us but paid no attention. Both Jan and I were walking with difficulty, he with a badly bruised leg and myself with this stabbing burning pain that came with every breath and every movement. This was not unusual, though; a number of slaves were crippled in various ways. The third Master had been dragged behind the machines to lie with the other two. It was almost time for the other one to return from the garden pool. He would find them, and perhaps raise an alarm, but the machines would be running as usual, and pure water emerging. The contaminated water was already on its way through the pipes to faucets all over the City.

We put a good distance between ourselves and the purification plant. We went to a communal place, to freshen up. I drank water, but it tasted no different. From tests on Ruki, the scientists had worked out that quite a minute proportion of alcohol had a paralyzing effect on them, but I wondered now if what we had managed to put in was enough. With our masks off, Fritz ran his hands over the upper part of my body. I winced, and almost cried out.

"A fractured rib," he said. "I thought so. We will try to make it more comfortable."

There were spare masks in the communal place. He ripped one up, and used the material to make two bandages, which he fixed above and below the place where it hurt most. He told me to breathe out as far as possible. Then he tightened and knotted the bandages. It hurt more while he was doing it, but I felt better after that.

We waited half an hour before going out. The Masters were tremendous consumers of water, never going longer than an hour without drinking. We walked about, and watched, but nothing seemed to have changed. They passed us with their usual arrogance, their contemptuous disregard. I began to feel despondent again.

Then, passing a pyramid, we saw one of them come out. Mario gripped my arm, unthinkingly, and I winced. But the pain did not matter. The Master teetered on his three stubby legs, his tentacles moved uncertainly. A moment later, he crashed and lay still.

6
The Pool of Fire

I do not know what they thought was happening to them, but they plainly failed to work it out. Perhaps they thought it was the Sickness, the Curse of the Skloodzi, operating in a new and more virulent fashion. I suppose the notion of poisoning was something they were incapable of grasping. They had, as we had found with Ruki, an apparently infallible means of sensing anything in their food or drink which could be injurious. Apparently infallible, but not quite. It had to be defensive toward a danger which you have never imagined existed.

So they drank and staggered, and fell; a few at first and then more and more until the streets were littered with their grotesque and monstrous bodies. The slaves moved among them, pitifully at a loss, occasionally trying to rouse them, timid and imploring at the same time. In a plaza where more than a score of Masters were lying, a slave rose from beside one of the men, his face streaming tears. He called out, "The Masters are no more. Therefore our lives no longer have a purpose. Brothers, let us go to the Place of Happy Release together."

Others moved toward him gladly. Fritz said,

"I think they would do it, too. We must stop them."

Mario said, "How? Does it matter, anyway?"

Not answering, Fritz jumped onto a small platform of stone, which was sometimes used by one of the Masters for a kind of meditation they did. He cried, "No, brothers! They are not dead. They sleep. Soon they will wake, and need our care."

They were irresolute. The one who had urged them before said, "How do you know this?"

"Because my Master told me, before it happened."

It was a clincher. Slaves might lie to each other, but never about anything relating to the Masters. The idea was unthinkable. Bewildered, but a little less sorrowful, they dispersed.

As soon as it was apparent that the scheme had succeeded, we turned to the second and equally important part of our task. The paralysis, as we knew, was temporary. It might have been possible, I suppose, to kill each Master individually as he lay helpless, but we probably would not find them all in the time . . . quite apart from the fact that it was most unlikely that the slaves would permit us to do it. As long as the Masters were not dead, but only unconscious, the power of the Caps remained.

The answer was to strike at the heart of the City, and wreck it. We knew — it was one of the first things Fritz had discovered — where the machines were that controlled the City's power:

its heat and light and the force that produced this dragging leaden weight under which we labored. We headed in that direction. It was some way off, and Carlos suggested we should use the horseless carriages which carried the Masters about. Fritz vetoed that. Slaves drove the carriages for their Masters, but did not use them otherwise. The Masters were in no position to notice the infringement, but the slaves would, and we did not know how they would react to it.

So we toiled along to Street 11, and to Ramp 914. The approach was through one of the biggest plazas in the City, lined with many ornate garden pools. The ramp itself was very broad and dipped underground in front of a pyramid that towered above its neighbors. From beneath came a hum of machinery that made the ground under our feet vibrate slightly. I had a sense of awe, going down into the depths. It was a place that the slaves never approached, and so we had not been able to. This was the City's beating heart, and we a handful of pygmies daring to approach it.

The ramp led into a cavern twice or three times as big as any I had seen, made up of three half-circles about a central circle. In each of the hemispheres there were huge banks of machinery, having hundreds of incomprehensible dials along the front. Scattered about the floor were the bodies of the Masters who had tended them. Some, clearly, had dropped at their posts.

I saw one whose tentacle was still curled about a lever.

The number of the machines, and their complexity, confused us. I looked for switches by which they might be turned off, but found none. The metal, gleaming a faint bronze, was unyielding and seamless, the dials covered by toughened glass. We went from one to another, looking for a weak spot but finding nothing. Was it possible that, even with the Masters made potent, their machines, ceaselessly humming, would continue to defy us?

Fritz said, "Perhaps that pyramid in the middle . . ."

It occupied the dead center of the inner circle. The sides were about thirty-five feet at the base and formed equilateral triangles, so that the apex was more than thirty feet high. We had not paid much attention to it before because it did not look like a machine, being featureless, apart from a single triangular doorway, high enough to admit a Master. But there were no fallen bodies anywhere near it.

It was of the same bronze metal as the machines, but we did not hear a hum as we approached. Instead there was a faint hissing noise, rising and falling in volume and also in tone. The doorway showed only more blank metal inside. There was a pyramid within the pyramid, with an empty space between them. We walked along the passage this formed and found the inner pyramid also had a doorway, but in a different face.

We went through, and found ourselves facing a third pyramid inside the second!

This, too, had a doorway, but in the side which was blank in the containing pyramids. A glow came from within. We entered, and I stared in awe.

A circular pit took up most of the floor, and the glow was coming from there. It was golden, something like the golden balls produced in the Sphere Chase, but deeper and brighter. It was fire, but a liquid fire, pulsing in a slow rhythm which matched the rise and fall of the hissing sound. One had an impression of power — effortless, unceasing, great enough to provide energy for the whole of this vast City.

Fritz said, "This is it, I think. But how does one stop it?"

Mario said, "On the far side . . . do you see?"

It lay beyond the glow, a single slim column, about the height of a man. Something protruded from the top. A lever? Mario, not waiting for an answer, was going around the glowing pit toward it. I saw him reach up, touch the lever — and die.

He made no sound, and perhaps did not know what was happening to him. Pale fire ran down the arm grasping the lever, divided and multiplied to leap in a dozen different streams along his body. He stayed like that for a brief instant before slumping. I saw the lever come down with his dead weight before his fingers unclasped and he slipped to the ground.

There was a shocked murmur from the others. Carlos moved, as though to go to him. Fritz said, "No. It would do no good, and might kill you, too. But, look! At the pit."

The glow was dying. It went slowly, as though reluctantly, the depths remaining lambent while the surface first silvered and then darkened over. The hissing faded, slowly, slowly, and this time into a whisper that trailed into silence. Deep down the glow reddened to a dull crimson. Spots of blackness appeared, increased in size, and ran together. Until at last we stood there, in silence and in the pitch dark.

In a low voice, Fritz said, "We must get out. Hold on to each other."

At that moment, the ground shuddered under us, almost as though we were in a minor earthquake. And suddenly we were liberated from the oppressive leaden weight which had dragged at us throughout our time here. My body was light again. It felt as though thousands of little balloons, attached to nerves and muscles, were lifting me up. It is an odd thing. For all the sensation of lightness and airiness, I found myself desperately weary.

We shuffled and groped our way through the maze of pyramids, blind leading the blind. In the great cavern it was just as black, the light having gone out. Black and silent, for there was no hum of machines any longer. Fritz guided us to what he thought was the entrance, but instead we came up against one of the banks of machines.

We went along, feeling the metal with our hands. Twice he checked, encountering the body of a Master, and once I myself, at the end of the line, unwittingly put my foot on the end of a tentacle. It rolled nauseatingly under my foot, and I wanted to be sick.

At last we found the entrance and, making our way along the curving ramp, saw the glimmer of green daylight ahead. We went more quickly, and soon could let go of each other. We came out, into the great plaza with the garden pools. I saw a couple of Masters floating in one of them, and wondered if they had drowned. It really did not matter any longer.

Three figures confronted us at the next intersection. Slaves. Fritz said, "I wonder . . ."

They looked dazed, as though knowing themselves to be in a dream — on the point of waking but not capable of bringing themselves into full consciousness. Fritz said, "Greetings, friends."

One of them answered, "How do we get out of this . . . place? Do you know a way?"

It was an ordinary, simple remark, but it told us everything. No slave would possibly seek a way out of the hellish paradise in which they could serve the Masters. It meant that the control was broken, the Caps they wore over their skulls as powerless as the ones we had put on for a disguise. These were free men. And if this were the case inside the City, it must be equally true in the world beyond. We were a fugitive minority no longer.

"We will find one," Fritz said. "You can help us."

We talked with them as we made our way toward the Hall of the Tripods, the gateway to the City. They were desperately confused, as was natural. They remembered what happened since they were Capped, but could make no sense of it. Their earlier selves, who had gladly and worshipfully tended the Masters, were strangers to them. The horror of what they had experienced was slow in dawning, but searing when it came. Once they all three stopped, where two Masters had fallen side by side, and I thought they might be going to savage them. But, after a long moment's looking, they turned their heads away, shuddering, and walked on.

We met many of the Capped. Some joined our party; others wandered aimlessly about, or sat staring into vacancy. Two were shouting nonsense, perhaps turned Vagrant by the withdrawal of the Masters' influence as some had been by its imposition. A third, who possibly had gone the same way, was lying at the edge of one of the ramps. He had taken his mask off, and his face wore a hideous grimace of death: he had choked in the poisonous green air.

Our band was some thirty strong when we came to the spiral ramp, at the edge of the City, which rose to the platform that fronted the Entering Place. I remembered coming down, on my first day here, trying to keep upright on knees that buckled under me. We reached the platform, and were on a height above the smaller pyramids. There was the door, through which we had come from the changing room. On the other side of it, air that we could breathe. I was ahead of the others, and pressed the small button which had worked the entrance to the air lock. Nothing happened. I pressed again, and again. Fritz had come up. He said, "We should have realized. The power for all the City came from the pool of fire. For the carriages, and also for opening and closing doors. It will not work now."

We took turns to hammer and bang against the barrier, but utterly without success. Someone found a piece of metal, and tried that; it dented the surface, but the door would not yield. One of the newcomers said, fear very plain in his voice, "Then we are trapped in here!"

Could it be so? The sky was less bright, as the afternoon faded. In a few hours it would be night, and the City dark and lightless. The heat was no longer as powerful, without the machines to maintain it. I wondered if cold would kill the Masters, or if they might recover before it reached that point. And, recovering, relight the pool of fire . . . Surely, we could not be defeated now.

I thought of something else, too. If this air lock would not open, neither would those on the communal places inside the pyramids. We had no means of getting food or water. More important, no means of renewing the filters in our masks. We would choke to death, as that one lying on the ramp had done. I had an idea, from the look on Fritz's face, that the same thought had come to him.

The one who was hammering with the metal said, "I think it will give if we persist long enough. If you others found things to hammer with, as well."

Fritz said, "It would not help much. There is the other door beyond that. Then the Entering Place. The room that goes up and down will not be working, either. We could never get past that. There will be no light in there . . ."

Silence registered agreement with what he had said. The one with the metal stopped hammering. We stood in a motionless dispirited group. Carlos looked up at the vast crystal bubbles, a translucent green dome covering the maze of ramps and pyramids.

"If we could only get up there," he said, "and knock a hole in that . . ."

Jan sat down, to test his injured leg. He said, "You can stand on my shoulders, if you like."

It was a feeble joke, and no one laughed. No one was in a mood for laughing. I drew a deep breath, and winced at the pain in my bandaged ribs. I was trying to think of something, but all my brain would say was: "Trapped . . . trapped."

Then one of the Capped said, "There is a way up."

"How can there be?"

"My . . ." He hesitated. "One of — them — showed me. He was inspecting the dome, and I had to take things up to him. A way up, and a ledge running around, inside the dome, at the top of the Wall."

I said, "We could never hope to break through the dome. It must be stronger than the glass over the dials on the machines. I doubt if we could even scratch its surface."

"We're going to try, though," Fritz said. "I see no other way out except by the river."

I had forgotten the river! I looked at him happily.

"Of course! Well, why not do that? Escape through the river?"

"I am not sure you would make it, Will, battered as you are. But we can't, anyway. We have to be sure they aren't able to take over again, when they recover consciousness. We must wreck the City while we have the chance."

I nodded, my happiness disappearing as rapidly as it had come. The river was no answer.

We went down the ramp again, this time with our new guide leading the way. At one of the garden pools, we equipped ourselves with metal stakes: they had been used for training a certain creeping plant that ran along the edges of the pools, and we could wrench them out without too much difficulty. Coming away, I thought I saw one of the fallen Masters stir. It was hardly anything, just the quiver of a tentacle, but the sight was ominous. I spoke to Fritz about it, and he nodded, and told the guide to move faster.

The way up, of which he had spoken, was in a part of the City filled with tall tapering pyramids — one to which the slaves had very rarely gone. This was a ramp, too, but one which clung to the Wall; narrow, and vertiginously steep. He had warned us of that, and said that he did not know how he had climbed it on that earlier occasion — that he could not have done it if he had not had a direct order from the Master. The ending of their gravity made it less difficult physically, but as we climbed higher and higher, and an unfenced abyss yawned beside and beneath us, the sensation was a terrifying one. I kept in as close to the gleaming surface of the Wall as I could and, after one horrified glimpse, did my best to avoid looking down.

We reached the ledge at last. It too was unfenced, and no more than four feet wide. The Masters must have had no sensitivity to heights. It ran along inside the Wall as far as the eye could see in either direction. The edge of the crystal bubble came down to within about eight feet of it. For one of the Masters, of course, this would be below eye level, but for us . . .

We had a try. Some made backs for the others, who clambered up and wielded their stakes awkwardly. I could not, because of my ribs, but it was harrowing enough having to watch them. The ledge seemed to shrink, and an incautious movement precipitated the fear of their falling down to the ground, two or three hundred feet below. They slammed at the crystal, and at the point where it joined with the metal of the Wall. But there was no sign of a seam, they said, and no sign of their blows making any impression at all. A second team was formed farther along, and a third, but with no greater success.

Fritz said, "Stop a minute." To the one who had guided us, he went on, "You met your Master here?"

He shook his head. "No, I did not see him. The command was to bring food and gas bubbles and leave them here. I stayed no longer than was necessary."

"You did not even see him farther along the ledge?"

"No, but he might have been out of sight. One cannot see across to the far side."

"One cannot see through the Wall, either."

"They could not live out there, in ordinary air. And he did not have a mask with him."

Fritz said, "They would need to be able to inspect the outside as well as the inside. It's worth searching for." He looked up at the sweep of crystal, with the pale disk of the sun well down toward the west. "Unless someone has a better idea."

No one had. We set out to walk along the ledge, in a clockwise direction. On our right was the precipitous fall to the City's streets. Some of the smaller pyramids looked like spikes, ready to impale that body that dropped on them. I felt sick from the height, and my chest was hurting badly again. I supposed I could have dropped out, and gone back; it was not as though I were going to be any use to anyone in my condition. But the thought of turning back, of leaving my companions, was worse still.

We trailed on. The top of the ramp was lost in the haze behind us. There was nothing to find, I was sure. The Master would have simply been out of sight, as we now were. Then, from the front, Fritz said, "There is something!"

The others were obscuring my view, but after a moment I saw what he meant. Just ahead, the ledge ended, or rather was replaced by something which projected out from the Wall to take up its full space and more. A sort of blockhouse — and with a door. But the door did not have a button to operate it. Instead there was a wheel, of the same golden metal as the Wall itself.

We crowded up, ignoring vertigo for the moment, as Fritz tried to turn the wheel. He got nowhere at first, but then, trying it in the reverse direction, it moved. Not much but enough to give us hope. He swung on it again, using all his strength, and it yielded a bit more. After a few minutes, he handed over to another. This continued, with volunteers working in relays. The wheel moved painfully slowly, but it went on moving. And, at last, we saw a crack widen in the side. The door was opening to us.

As soon as the gap was wide enough, Fritz

squeezed through, and we followed. I was glad, in view of my bandaged ribs, that I was smaller than the average. There was light, from the partly opened door and also from squares of crystal in the roof. We could see our surroundings quite clearly.

The blockhouse was slotted into the Wall, and existed on either side of it. It was very bare, but held some boxes, which probably contained equipment, and, on a rack, half a dozen of the mask-suits which the Masters could wear if they had to breathe human air.

Fritz pointed to them:

"That was why he did not take a mask. They were kept here." He looked round the cell-like room. "They would not bring power all the way up here. It would not be worth it. So the doors open mechanically. All the doors."

There was one facing the one through which he had come, presumably leading out to a continuation of the ledge. At the far side, two similar doors faced each other. They must open onto a similar ledge, but one outside the dome. I said, "But if this is an air lock . . . you would need power for pumping the air."

"I do not think so. Remember, their air is denser, under greater pressure than ours. A simple valve, worked by pressure, would do it. And the amount of air in here, compared with the amount under the dome, is terribly small. It would not matter."

Jan said, "So all we have to do is open one of

the doors, on the outside. What are we waiting for?"

Fritz put his hands on the wheel, tensed, and heaved to the right. His powerful muscles bulged with the strength he was applying. He relaxed, and heaved again. Nothing happened. He stood back, wiping his brow.

"Someone else try."

Several others did so.

Carlos said, "This is ridiculous. The door is the same as the other. The wheel is identical."

Fritz said, "Wait a minute. I think maybe I understand. Close the inner door."

A wheel inside matched the outer one. It turned, though with the same reluctance: these had been made for Masters' strength, not human. At last, it was sealed.

"Now," Fritz said.

He heaved on the outer door's wheel again. This time it moved. Slowly, slowly, but at last there was a crack of light, and the crack widened. There was the whistling noise of air escaping, the breeze of its passing on our bodies. Ten minutes later, we were looking out onto a ledge, the outside of the dome, and the earthly landscape that was spread out below us, a patchwork of fields, and streams, and the distant hump of the ruined great-city. The brightness of daylight made us blink our eyes.

Fritz said, "Even the Masters can make mistakes, so they have a device to prevent that happening here. The doors to the outside will not open unless the doors to the inside are sealed. And the other way around, I should think. Try to open the inner door now."

An attempt was made, and failed. It was obvious that what he said was right.

Carlos said, "Then we can open one door . . . but must smash a way through the other?"

Fritz was examining the open door.

"That will not be easy. Look at it."

The door was about four inches thick, made of the tough gleaming metal that formed the Wall. It had been machined to a satiny smoothness and, obviously, to such a precision that even air would not pass between the opposing surfaces when it was sealed. Fritz picked up the spike he had been carrying and hammered at it. It made no impression that I could see.

We had come to another, perhaps a final check. We could keep the inner door closed and thus, with our own air surrounding us, we could remove the masks. So we would not suffocate. But we had no food here, no water — above all, no means of getting down the sheer shining cliff of the Wall. In any case, unless we could puncture the City's shell in some way, we faced the possibility of the Masters recovering from their paralysis and restarting the pool of fire.

We were all looking at the door. Carlos said, "There is a difference between the inner doors and the outer ones. The first one opened inward, but this opens out."

Fritz shrugged. "Because of the difference in

pressure. It makes it easier for them."

Carlos squatted, fingering the place where door and wall joined.

"The door itself is too strong to be broken. But the hinges . . ."

Hinges ran all the way up the inside, thin and bright and gleaming a little with oil. Renewed, perhaps, by the Master who had unwittingly led us this far.

Fritz said, "I think we could break them. But we can only get at them with the doors open, which means the inner door is sealed. How does that help?"

"Not break them entirely," Carlos said. "But if we were to weaken them — then close the door — then, after opening the inner door . . ."

"Try to hammer it open from inside? It might work! At any rate, we can try."

They got down to it, two at a time hammering at the joints of the hinges. It was still not easy, but a cry of triumph told us that the first had broken. Others followed. They went through them systematically, leaving only a single hinge at the top and one at the bottom untouched. Then the door was wound shut again, and the inner door opened.

"Right," Fritz said. "Now we hammer, top and bottom."

They banged and thumped with the metal stakes. Fritz and Carlos had started; when they were exhausted they passed the task on to others. These, in turn, tired, and were replaced.

Minutes dragged by, to the monotonous unchanging clang of metal on metal. The crystal squares in the roof were darkening, dusk beginning to fall. I wondered if the Masters were stirring down in the streets, moving about, in confusion but with a purpose . . . making their way toward the dark pit where the fire had danced, and still might dance . . . I said, "Can I have a go?"

"I'm afraid you would not be much help," Fritz said. "All right, Carlos. You and I once more."

The hammering went on and on. Then my ear caught something else, a sort of creak. It came again, and again.

"Harder!" Fritz called.

There was a sound of metal tearing. The two hinges must have given way almost simultaneously. The door began to fall, and I glimpsed the open sky, graying now. That was the last thing I noticed clearly for quite a time. Because, as the door collapsed outward, a great wind swept through the blockhouse, from open door to open door, a gale plucking one outward. Someone shouted, "Get down!" I dropped to the floor, and it was a little better there. I felt it tearing at my back, but I stayed where I was. It roared through, and it was like no noise of wind I had ever heard because it stayed on one note, unvarying, a harsh unending bellow. I wondered that I could have thought the hammering monotonous. One could not speak above the din, even if one had not been too dazed to have anything to say. I could see the others scattered on the floor. It was incredible that it could go on for so long, unchanging.

But change came at last. The noise was covered by another, sharper, far louder, more terrifying. It sounded as though the sky itself was splitting and tearing to shreds. And a moment later, the wind died. I was able to get groggily to my feet, only now realizing that my ribs were hurting even more because of my drop to the floor.

Several of us went to the inner doorway. We looked out silently, too awed for comment. The crystal dome had shattered inward. Quite a lot still adhered to the top of the Wall, but a jagged hole extended all across the center. Huge shards could be seen, where they had fallen on the City; one seemed to be covering the Sphere Arena. I turned to look for Fritz. He was standing alone by the outer door.

I said, "That's it. Not one of them could have survived."

There were tears in his eyes, and one rolled down his cheek. Of joy, I thought at first, but there was no joy in his expression. I asked, "What's the matter, Fritz?"

"Carlos . . ."

He gestured toward the open door. I said, in horror, "No!"

"The wind plucked him through. I tried to hold him, but could not."

We looked out together. The Wall was a precipice beneath our feet. Far, far down, a tiny square of gold marked the position of the door. Near it lay a small black speck . . .

We ripped off the masks, and could breathe ordinary air. The green air of the Masters had spread out and been lost in the vastness of the world's ordinary atmosphere. We made our way back along the ledge, and down the steep ramp into the City. I was glad we had not left it any later than this; light was fading rapidly and lack of visibility did nothing to improve my sense of dizziness. But we got down at last.

The communal places were still barred to us, inside the pyramids. We found stores of food, though, in open warehouses, and broke open the crates to eat it. There were drinking fountains in several places, put there to serve the thirst of passing Masters, and we drank from them. The bodies of the Masters themselves lay scattered about in the growing dark. We were joined by more and more of the Capped. They were shaken and bewildered, and some had been injured by fragments of the falling dome; we cared for them as best we could. Then we settled down to endure a cold spring night. It was not pleasant, but at least the stars shone overhead, the diamond-bright stars of earth.

In the morning, shivering, Fritz and I discussed what to do. We still could not get through the Entering Place without a slow and arduous business of breaking down doors, and the door in the Wall, that opened to admit the Tripods, would be a well-nigh impossible proposition. We could escape by way of the river, of course, but that, too, would not be easy — in my case, suicidal. I said, "We could tie things together to make a rope — there are stocks of the material they use to make clothes for the slaves — let ourselves down the blockhouse . . ."

"It would take a long rope," he said. "I think it might be worse than the river. But I've been wondering . . ."

"What?"

"All the Masters are dead. If we were to start the pool of fire again . . ."

"How? Remember Mario."

"I do. The power killed him. But that switch was meant to be used."

"By a tentacle. They are of a different substance to our flesh. Perhaps the power does not run through it. Are we to chop off a tentacle, and use it to push the lever up again?"

"It is an idea," he said, "but not what I had in mind. The fire was on when Mario grasped the lever. It died slowly. If it also starts slowly . . . Do you see what I mean? There might be no danger until the fire is burning."

I said slowly, "You could be right. I'll do it."

"No," Fritz said decisively. "I will."

We went down the ramp into the Hall of the Machines. The darkness was absolute, and we had to guess our way toward the central pyramid. There was a strange smell, rather like rotting leaves, and when I had the misfortune to stumble over the body of one of the Masters I realized where it was coming from. They were beginning to decompose, and I suppose it was worse down here than out in the streets.

We missed the pyramid completely the first time, and came up against the banks of machines in one of the hemispheres beyond. Our second attempt was more successful. I touched smooth metal, and called to Fritz to join me. Together we felt our way around to the side with the entrance, and through the maze of concentric pyramids. It was no darker here, of course, than anywhere else in the Hall, but I was more afraid. The confinement, perhaps, had something to do with it — that, and the fact that we were approaching the pit where the fire had burned.

As we came to the third entrance, Fritz said, "You stay here, Will. Come no farther."

I said, "Don't be silly. Of course I'm coming."

"No." His voice was flat and final. "It is you that are being silly. If anything goes wrong, you are in charge. A safe way out of the City will still need to be found."

I was silent, recognizing the truth of what he said. I could hear him edging his way around, avoiding the central pit. It took a long time, because he went cautiously. At last, he said, "I have reached the column. I am feeling for the switch now. I have got it. I have pushed it up!"

"You are all right? Get away from it, just in case."

"I have done that. But nothing is happening. There is no sign of the fire."

Nor was there. I strained my eyes into blackness. Perhaps it had been out for too long. Perhaps there was something else that needed doing, which we could not begin to guess at. His voice showing his disappointment, Fritz said, "I'm on my way back."

I put a hand out, and reached him. He said, "It will have to be the rope, or the river. It is a pity. I had hoped we might control the City."

I thought at first it might be my eyes playing tricks with me, showing spots of brilliance as they sometimes do in darkness. I said, "Wait . . ." And then, "Look!"

He turned with me, and we both stared. Down in what must be the bottom of the pit, a spark flicked into being followed by another and another. They grew, ran together, began glowing brightly. The fire spread and leaped as we watched, and the hissing noise began. Then the whole pit was shimmering with it, as the radiance filled the room.

7

A Summer on the Wind

The Masters were dead, but the City lived again.

The leaden weight dragged at us as before, but we did not mind that. In the Hall outside, the green lamps glowed, and the machines hummed with their ceaseless mysterious activity. We went up to the streets and, finding a carriage, climbed in and drove along to where we had left the others. They stood and goggled at us. At the perimeter of the City, a green fog was rising, showing that the machine which produced the Masters' air had also begun working again. But it did not appear to be a danger. It rose up through the shattered dome, and was lost in the sky's blue immensity.

We collected what followers we could, and set out once more for the Entering Place. This time, the door worked at the touch of a button. Inside, we found the Capped whose duty had been to prepare new slaves. They were bewildered, and the air was not good after eighteen hours, but otherwise they were all right. It was they who showed us how to operate the room that moved, and the opening of the Wall.

I said, "Tripods . . . Many of them will have been caught outside. They may be waiting there.

If we open up . . ."

"Waiting for what?" Fritz said. "They know that the dome is wrecked."

"If the Tripods come in, the Masters in them may have masks. And the machine that makes their air is still working. They could do something — perhaps start to repair things."

Fritz turned to the one who had showed us how the Wall was made to open. He said, "The Hall of Tripods has human air. How did they get into the part where they could breathe?"

"The Masters' door in the hemispheres fitted against ports high up in the inner part of the Hall. They could step through."

"Did the ports open from the outside?"

"No. From here. We pressed a button to open them when the Masters commanded us." He pointed to a grille in the wall. "Their voices came through that, though they themselves were outside in the Tripods."

"You will stay here," Fritz said, "with a few others that you can choose. Later, you will be relieved, but until then your duty will be to see the ports are kept closed. Is that understood?"

He spoke with the authority of someone that expects obedience, and his order was accepted without demur. The four of us left from the six who had invaded the City were treated altogether with deference and respect. Even though the Caps no longer had an effect on their minds, they felt awe at the thought of our having fought against the Masters, and defeated them.

The rest of us went down through the room that moved, and came out into the Hall of the Tripods. The green lamps were on, but their light was lost in the daylight that poured through the open section of the Wall, a gap more than fifty feet wide and more than twice that in height. Ranks of Tripods stretched away along the Hall, but motionless, and presumably untenanted. In their presence we were pygmies again, but triumphant pygmies. We walked through the opening, and Jan clutched my arm. Another Tripod stood there, looking menacingly down at us.

Fritz cried, "Prepare to scatter! As widely as you can, if it attacks. It cannot catch us all."

But the tentacles hung flaccidly from the hemisphere. The menace was an illusion. There was no life there. After a few moments we knew this was so, and our tension relaxed. We walked, unconcerned, under its shadow, and some of those who had been Capped climbed up on one of the great metal feet, and shouted and laughed for joy.

Fritz said to me, "I should have thought they would have enough air, and food and water, to last longer than that. In fact, they must have, since they go on journeys that last for days, or even weeks."

"Does it matter?" I said, "They are dead." I was tempted to join those clambering on the Tripod's foot, but knew that it would be childish. "Perhaps they died of broken hearts!" (And perhaps my silly guess was not so far from the truth. We found later that all the Tripods had stopped working within a few hours of the fire going out in the City. Our scientists examined the bodies of the Masters inside. It was impossible to tell how they had died, but it may have been through despair. Their minds were not like ours. Ruki, however, did not die — not then. Perhaps because, having grown used to captivity, he could better withstand the shock of the City's fall, and live on in hope of eventual rescue.)

The day was bright, as though in celebration of our victory. Great fluffy clouds hung white in the heavens, but the areas of blue were larger still and the sun was rarely hidden. The breeze was slight, but warm, and smelled of growing things and of the spring. We made our way around the Wall's circumference, back to the river and the outpost from which we had set out. Figures waved to us as we approached, and I realized again that the days of hiding and subterfuge were over. It seemed that the earth was ours.

André was there. He said, "Good work! We thought you might be trapped inside."

Fritz told him about restarting the pool of fire and he listened intently.

"That's even better. The scientists will go mad with delight over that. It means their secrets are open to us."

I stretched, and then winced as I was reminded of my ribs. I said, "They'll have time enough to study them. We can take things easy now."

"Not easy," André said. "We have won here, but there may be counterattacks."

"From the other Cities?" Fritz asked. "How long will it be before we have news from them?"

"We have it already."

"But the pigeons could not travel so fast."

"The invisible rays are much faster than pigeons. Although we dared not use them to transmit messages, we have been listening to those the Masters sent. They have stopped from two Cities, but are still coming from the third."

"The one in the east?" I suggested. "The little yellow men failed then . . ."

"No, not that," André said. "The one in the west."

That was the attack in which Henry would have taken part. I thought of him, and of the two we had lost, and the bright day seemed to cloud over.

But Henry was still alive. Two months later, at the castle, he told the other three of us — Fritz, Beanpole, and me — about it.

From the start, things had gone wrong for them. Two of their six had developed, at the last minute, a sickness which was common among humans in that part; and their places had been taken by two others who were less well trained. One of these had got into difficulties during their attempt to swim up the underground tunnel, forcing them to turn back and try again the following night. Even when they had gained access to the City, there were irritating setbacks and delays. They had difficulty in finding a warehouse with sufficient supplies of starch foods to make the mash for fermentation, and when they did succeed their first efforts were failures, because some of the yeasts would not grow. They had also been unable to find a hideout within close reach of the water purification plant, which meant a lot of exhausting transportation of the liquor by night.

But they had reached their quota by the time appointed, and Henry thought it would be easy from that point. Although our attempt had to be made at midday, they were able to start theirs at dawn, before the first duty shift of Masters came on. Or, at least, they thought they could. The way to the ramp leading down to the water purification plant, however, as in the City which we had tackled, was through an open place with garden pools, and they found that one of them was occupied by two Masters.

They looked as though they were wrestling, pushing and tugging at each other with their tentacles, threshing the water and sending up gouts of spray. Fritz and I had seen a similar thing, during the night when we were searching for the river and a way out of the City. We had made nothing of it — it was one of the many strange habits of the Masters over which the scientists had shaken their heads — and Henry did not, either. All he could do was hope that, whatever it was, they would soon put an end to it and go away. But they did not, and time was passing, whittling away the minutes that remained before the first day shift would arrive.

In the end, deliberately, he took a chance. The two Masters seemed entirely preoccupied and they were in the pool farthest from the ramp. He decided to have his men worm their way along the wall that enclosed the second pool, and then dash for the ramp where the shadows were deepest. Three did so successfully, but the fourth must have been seen. With a surprising swiftness, the Masters heaved themselves out of the pool and came to investigate.

They killed one, and would have killed the other, he thought, if he had stood his ground. But this one had actually seen the incredible happen — Masters attacked by slaves — and went spinning from the scene, howling in his own peculiar language. He would obviously return with others: there was no hope of getting more than half a dozen containers of alcohol in the culvert before he did so, and that would mean the Masters alerted to the danger. Not only there, perhaps, but in the other two Cities as well; for the messages would go to them immediately on the invisible rays.

The enterprise had failed, and they must cut their losses. Avoiding capture, and the baring of their thoughts, must be the objective now — at least long enough for the attacks on the other two Cities to go through. Henry told his men to scatter, and himself set off through the warren of the City's streets and ramps, heading for the river exit.

He got through, and so did two others. He had no idea of what had happened to the remaining three, but thought they must have been captured: they had watched the river for their bodies, but found nothing. (It was not a true river but a creation of the ancients — a huge canal cut across land to connect the western ocean with the even vaster ocean on the far side of the isthmus.) There had been great activity by patrolling Tripods, but they had lain low in an underground refuge and had escaped detection. Eventually, they had managed to get away, to the ship and so back here.

"A miserable failure altogether," he concluded.

"You had bad luck," I said. "We all needed good luck to succeed, and you didn't have it."

"It was not a failure, even," Fritz said. "Whatever happened to those you lost, they must have dodged capture until it was too late. No warning came to the other Cities."

Beanpole said: "I was with Julius when the news arrived. He said he would have been pleased if we had taken one City. Two was more than anyone could have hoped for."

Henry said, "That doesn't alter the fact that they have the continent of the Americans still. What do we do now? We wouldn't have much chance of getting in as spies again. They may not know quite what went wrong, but they certainly won't trust any human slaves in future."

I said, "I can't understand why they have not counterattacked."

"They may still do so," Fritz said.

"They're leaving it a bit late. If they had been able to set up another transmitter over here before we fixed the Caps, they would have made things much more difficult for us."

The Caps, which were woven into the very flesh of those who wore them, could not be removed, but our scientists had found how to damage the mesh so that they would no longer serve their old purpose. We, for our part, had been able to take off the false-Caps which we had worn as disguise; it was wonderful not to have metal pressing against one's skull.

Fritz said: "I think maybe they have decided to concentrate on defense. Their Cities here and in the east are destroyed, and they can do nothing about that. In a year and a half, the great ship will come from their home planet. They probably think that they only have to hold out until then. As long as they still have one continent, they can set up the machines to poison our air."

Henry said restlessly, "A year and a half . . . It's not long. Do you know what's being planned, Beanpole?"

Beanpole nodded. "Some of it."

"But I suppose you can't say?"

He smiled. "You'll know soon enough. I think Julius is going to break it to us at the banquet tomorrow."

The weather holding fine, the banquet was held in the courtyard of the castle. It was meant as a victory celebration, for those who had been concerned in the capture of the City, and we did very well indeed. We had all kinds of fish from the sea, and from the rivers trout and crayfish grilled in butter; followed by a choice of chicken and duck, suckling pig, pigeon pie, and cuts from an ox that had been roasted whole on a spit. There was also the sparkling wine of the north, which we had drunk at the banquet which followed the end of the Games. As impressive as the food and drink was the fact that we no longer had to go through the wearisome tasks of preparing the meal, setting up the tables and so on. We had servants now, and our food was brought to us. These were men who had been Capped. They treated us as heroes — all the Capped did — which was embarrassing but not unpleasant. The fact that the cooking was done by people who had been trained to the art was pure gain.

Julius spoke about the enterprise. His praise was circumspect rather than extravagant, but I found myself flushing as I listened to him. He singled Fritz out for special mention, as was right. It had been Fritz's steadiness and his resourcefulness which had pulled us through.

He went on, "You will have been wondering what comes next. We succeeded in destroying the Cities of the enemy here and in the east. But one City remains untaken, and as long as it stands the knife is at our throat. More than half the short time we had has passed. We must destroy that final citadel before their ship arrives.

"But at least, there is only one. A single assault, if properly organized and carried out, will bring us victory. And I may say that a plan for this is well advanced.

"It is based, as any with a hope of success must be, on the particular vulnerability which stems from the fact that they are alien to this world and must carry their own special environment with them to survive. In our first attacks, we drugged the Masters, and switched off the power which made the Cities work, but destruction only came about when the dome cracked, letting their air out and earthly air in. This is the way we must strike at the remaining City.

"There would be no point in trying to repeat the approach of sabotage from within. The latest news we have is that the Masters in the west have stopped recruiting Capped humans. We do not know what became of those already living as slaves in the City, but it is almost certain that they will have been killed, or commanded to kill themselves. No, we must attack from outside, and the question is: how?

"In the old days, as we have learned, men had means of obliterating stretches of territory as big as the City from halfway around the world. We could develop such things again, but not in the time which is left to us. We could produce a more primitive form of gun for throwing explosives, but it would not serve. Another report from across the ocean tells us that the Masters are laying waste the land for many miles both north and south, making sure that nothing can live there which might menace them. We need something else.

"And I believe we have it. There was one thing our ancestors achieved which the Masters seem never to have equaled. This was the construction of machines which could fly through the air. The Masters came from a planet whose heaviness must have made flight difficult, if not impossible. They went straight from surface travel to travel between worlds. Presumably they could, after conquering the earth, have copied the flying machines which were used here, but they did not do so. Perhaps out of some sort of pride, or because they thought the Tripods were good enough for their purposes . . . or because, through another quirk of their minds, they feared it."

I remembered my own fear and dizziness, climbing the ramp up the Wall and later walking along the narrow ledge high above the City's roofs. The Masters had obviously not felt like that or they would not have built in such a way. But there is not always rationality in fear. It could be that they were all right as long as they had some contact with the ground; terrified otherwise.

Julius said, "We have built flying machines . . ."

He said it plainly, without emphasis, but his words were lost in a spontaneous roar of applause from all of us.

Julius put his hand up for silence, but he was smiling.

"Not the sort of machines that the ancients built — machines which could carry hundreds of people across the western ocean in a few hours. Yes, you may gasp, but it is true. That sort of thing, like the machines for hurling destruction halfway around the world, is beyond our present reach. These are small and simple machines. But they do fly, and a man can ride in them and also carry explosives. They are what we shall use, and hope with that means to crack the enemy's last shell."

He went on to talk more generally. I had been expecting him to say something concerning our part in the new enterprise, but he did not. Later, when we were watching an exhibition by some jugglers, I asked him directly, "How soon do we start training on the flying machines, sir? And do we do it here, or in the land across the ocean?"

He looked at me with laughing eyes. "I should have thought you were too full to talk, Will, after the amount I have just seen you stuffing yourself with, let alone to think of flying through the air! How do you mange to eat so much and stay so small?"

"I don't know, sir. About the machines, though — they really have been built?"

"They have."

"So we can start learning to drive them soon?"

"We have men learning already. In fact, they have learned. It is a question of practicing now."

"But . . ."

"But what about your part in it? Listen, Will, a general does not use the same troops over and over again. You have done well, you and Fritz, and earned a respite."

"Sir! That was months ago. We've been doing nothing since then except live on the fat of the land. I would much rather start training on the flying machines."

"I am sure you would. But there is another thing a general has to do — he has to organize his men and his time. You do not wait for one operation to be over before starting the next. We dared not launch machines into the air while the City lived, but our men were studying them and studying old books about flying even then. The first machine went up the day after the City's dome exploded."

I argued, "But I could join them, and probably catch up. You've said I'm small. Isn't that a help? I mean, I would be less weight for the machines to carry."

He shook his head. "Weight is not so important. In any case, we have more than enough pilots. You know our rule, Will. Individual preferences do not matter: all that matters is what contributes to efficiency and so to success. The number of machines we have is limited, and therefore so are the facilities for training pilots.

Even if I thought you so much more suitable than those we already have — and in fact I don't — I would not approve something which meant that you would have to 'catch up' with others more advanced. It would not be an efficient thing to do."

He had spoken more firmly, to some extent in rebuke, and I had no choice but to accept his decision and put on as good a face as I could. Later, though, I told the story to Fritz, resentfully. He listened with his usual stolidness, and commented, "What Julius said is right, of course. You and I were included in the party that was to attack the City because we had lived in the City and had the advantage of knowing it. There is no such advantage in the case of the flying machines."

"So we have to stay here, messing about, doing nothing, while things happen on the other side of the ocean."

Fritz shrugged. "It seems so. And since there is no choice, we might as well make the best of it."

I am afraid I was not very good at doing this. I still felt that we could have caught up with those who had a start on us in driving the flying machines; and also that what we had done had earned us the right to be included in the final attack. I was hoping that Julius would change his mind, though that was not a thing that often happened. I only abandoned hope on the morning he rode out of the castle, on his way to another of our bases.

As I stood on the broken battlements, watching his horse jog away, Beanpole came to join me. He asked, "Nothing to do, Will?"

"There are plenty of things I could do. Swim, lie in the sun, catch flies . . ."

"Before he left, Julius gave me permission to start a project. You could help with it."

I said listlessly, "What is it?"

"Did I ever tell you about the time, before I met you, when I noticed that steam from a kettle rises, and I tried to make a balloon, which would go up in the air, and perhaps carry me?"

"I remember."

"I thought of floating away to a land where there were no Tripods. It didn't work, of course. For one thing, the air would cool and bring it down again pretty quickly. But when we were working on separating the gases in the air, to make those special masks so that you could swim upstream into the City, we also found how to make gases that are lighter than the air. If you fill a balloon with *those,* then it should go up and stay up. In fact, the ancients had them before they built flying machines."

I said, without much enthusiasm, "It sounds very interesting. What do you want me to do?"

"I've built a few balloons, and I've persuaded Julius to let me take a few people and see if we can get them working. We shall set up camp on our own and just — well, fly them, I suppose. Do you want to come? I've asked Henry and Fritz, and they're keen on it."

Under other circumstances, the idea would have fascinated me. At the moment, though, I saw it as putting a seal of finality on Julius's refusal to let me take part in the air attack on the third City, and very dull by comparison with that. I said, grudgingly, "I suppose so."

My resentment was childish, and, once I had finally accepted things, I quickly succeeded in pulling myself out of it. I was helped by the fact that ballooning was tremendous fun. We took the balloons on carts to a place inland where the country was wild and almost uninhabited — rough hilly land, the foothills of mountains which were less high than the White Mountains, but impressive enough. One of the things Beanpole wanted to learn was the way of maneuvering in different gusts and currents of air, and the hills provided plenty of these.

The balloon itself was of oilskin, but held in a mesh of silken cord which was attached in turn to the basket in which one traveled. The basket was staked to the ground before the balloon was filled with the light gas, and would bob there, straining against its ropes as though impatient to be up and away. The balloon was quite large, as much as ten feet across, and the basket large enough to carry four people, though two was our more usual crew. It also carried ballast — bags of sand which could be dropped to lighten the load in downdrafts.

Coming down was a relatively simple matter.

One pulled a cord which opened the balloon a little and let out some of the light gas. It was not at all difficult, but needed care: if it were pulled fully open, the balloon and basket would sink like a stone . . . not a pleasant prospect when the ground was hundreds of feet below you.

But this did not detract from the pleasure we got from it. I do not think I can recall anything so exhilarating as the first time I went up. I had left the ground before this, of course, plucked into the air by the tentacle of a Tripod, and that had been terrifying. Here, by contrast, everything was calm, and yet tremendously exciting. Beanpole cast off the last rope and we began to rise, quickly but smoothly and steadily. It was a calm afternoon, and we soared almost straight up toward a sky barred high up with white cirrus. Trees, bushes, the faces of those watching from the ground, dwindled and fell away. Every instant widened the vista we could see: the feeling was godlike. I felt that I never wanted to come down to earth again. How nice it would be if one could float through the skies forever, feeding on sunlight and drinking the rain from the clouds!

Gradually we became skilled in the handling of these huge bubbles which lifted us and carried us through the air. It was a more difficult art than one would have thought. Even on apparently calm days there were eddies, and at times the turbulence was wild. Beanpole talked of constructing much vaster balloons, which would have firm containing skins and engines to push them through the air, but that was a remote hope for the future. The craft we had now were entirely at the mercy of wind and weather. We had to learn to sail them like canoes passing down uncharted rivers where a stretch of sluggish calm might be followed, abruptly, around the next bend, by a savage tumble of rapids. We learned to know the sky, to read signs and portents in small things, to anticipate how a current of air would ride up the side of a rock face.

In this fascination I was able to forget, to some extent, that we were out of the struggle which must soon come to its crisis. The worst moment was when we were joined by some others from the castle, who told us that the men who would ride the flying machines had left to cross the ocean. They were traveling in a number of different ships for safety's sake, and each ship carried the parts that would be assembled, over there, to make the flying machines. Henry and I brooded over the news for a while. I discovered that he felt, if anything, worse than I did over being excluded — after all, he had actually been inside the third City and had seen his hopes of destroying it dashed.

But we could concentrate on our own useless and haphazard kind of flying — could rise high over the hills and look from an equal height at the brown summer peaks of the mountains. On the ground, we camped out and lived rough . . . but the roughness included catching our own fish in the rivers that tumbled down through bracken and heather and cooking them right away on hot embers. It included expeditions to trap not only rabbits and hares, but deer and wild pig, and subsequent feasting around a crackling fire in the dusk. After that, we slept soundly on the hard ground, and woke refreshed.

So the days and weeks and months went by. Summer passed, and the days shortened with the approach of autumn. It would soon be time to return to winter quarters at the castle. But a few days before we had expected to move, a messenger arrived there. The message was simple and bald: Julius wanted us back at once. We dismantled our balloons and packed them on the carts, and set off early next day, through a thin drizzle of rain.

I had never seen Julius look so strained and old. His eyes were tired, and I wondered how much he slept at night. I felt guilty about my own carefree days and nights up in the hills.

He said, "It is best to tell you right away. The news is bad. As bad as it can be."

Beanpole said, "The attack on the third City . . ."

". . . has failed utterly."

"What went wrong?"

"With the preparations, nothing. We got all the flying machines over safely, and established three bases, two in the north and one in the south. We disguised them, successfully it seemed, painting the machines so that from a distance, from a Tripod's height, they seemed to blend with the ground. It was a trick the ancients had used, in their wars, and it seemed to work. The Tripods did not molest them — gave no indication of knowing they were there. So, at the hour appointed, they set off, carrying their explosives toward the City."

Julius paused a moment. "Not one got within reach. All at once, their engines stopped."

Beanpole asked sharply, "Do we know why — how?"

"A part of the way the engines worked was through electricity. You will know more of that than I do. At the bases, miles farther back, everything electrical stopped at that same moment, but started again later on. A different kind of invisible ray, the scientists think, which kills all electrical things when it is used."

I said, "And the flying machines, sir? What happened to them?"

"Most of them crashed into the ground. A few managed to get down more or less intact. The Tripods came out from the City and destroyed them as they lay there, helpless."

Henry said, "All of them, sir?"

"Every one. The only flying machine we have left is one that would not start from its base because something was wrong with its engine."

Only now did the dire significance of what he had told us really sink in. I had been so sure that the attack would succeed, that these wonderful devices of the ancients would destroy the last stronghold of the enemy. Yet not only had the attack failed, the weapon on which our hopes were pinned had been blunted, and shown to be useless.

Beanpole said, "Well, sir?"

Julius nodded. "Yes. We are down to our last throw. Let us hope your balloons will pull us through."

I said to Beanpole, "You mean, you knew all the time that this was possible — that the balloons were something to fall back on if the flying machines failed?"

He looked at me with mild surprise. "But, of course. You do not think Julius would fail to have an alternative plan, right up to the last?"

"You might have told me."

He shrugged. "One leaves it to Julius to tell people what he thinks proper. And the balloons are a good project in themselves. The airships I spoke of — the ancients had something of the sort, but abandoned them for the heavy flying machines. I am not sure they were right to do that."

I said, "Do you know how soon we are to cross the ocean?"

"No. There are preparations to be made."

"Yes, of course."

He admonished me sharply, "Will, stop grinning like a fool. This is not designed for your benefit. It would have been better — infinitely better — if the attack by the flying machines had succeeded. As Julius said, this is our last chance."

I said penitently, "Yes, I realize that."

But penitence was not the feeling uppermost in my mind.

8

The Freedom Bubbles

We, too, and our balloons, were split between different ships for the journey across the ocean. Henry and I, though, found ourselves together, on a vessel of four or five hundred tons called *La Reine d'Azure.* The French sailors asked us, before we left harbor, if we would care to take some concoction of theirs which was designed to prevent seasickness. The sky, they said, promised dirty weather ahead. Henry accepted the offer, but I refused. The liquid looked doubtful, and smelled worse and, as I told them, I had crossed the seas before.

But that was a different sea — the narrow channel between my homeland and France — and in different conditions. We put out into choppy white-capped waves, with a wind from the east whipping spray along their tops. This was the wind we wanted, and all possible sail was crammed on to take advantage of it. *La Reine* swept along under a sky that steadily darkened, although it was not much past the middle of the day. A queen, perhaps, but a tipsy one, lurching from side to side, digging her bows into the troughs as the waves increased and deepened, and scattering foam as she came up again.

My own sensation was one of, at first, mild discomfort and I thought it would pass as I grew used to the motion. I stood by the bulwarks with Henry, wrapped up against the wind and wet, and talked cheerfully and cracked jokes. The discomfort, though, instead of passing, grew more insistent. One of the sailors who had offered me the seasickness remedy passed and asked me how I was. I laughed, and told him I was feeling fine — that it reminded me of the carousel that had been set up at the village fairs when I was a boy. The ship dropped, at that moment, from the crest of her upward swing down into horrific depths, and I shut my mouth and swallowed hastily. Fortunately, he had already gone.

From that point, the ship's battle with the waves was matched by another waged by my mind against my stomach. I was determined not to show what I was feeling even to Henry — my pride was stupidly engaged — and was relieved when he went below at the word that there was a hot drink waiting in the galley. He asked me if I were coming, and I shook my head, smiling desperately. I said, as was perfectly true, that I did not feel like a drink at that moment. So he left me, and I hung onto the rail, and stared at the sea, willing either it or my churning stomach to lie quiet. Neither did so. Time slowly passed, with nothing happening except that the sky was darker, the waves more extreme, the shuddering plunges and climbs of the *Reine d'Azure* more precipitous. My head was aching as well; but I hung on, and felt I must be winning.

Someone touched me from behind. Henry said, "You still here, Will? You're a glutton for fresh sea air."

I mumbled something, I don't know what. Henry continued, "I was talking to the captain. He says he thinks there might be some really rough weather ahead of us."

I turned, drawn by my incredulity over this remark. Really rough weather? I opened my mouth to say something and, on second thought, closed it again. Henry said solicitously, "Are you all right, Will? Your face is a funny color. A sort of olive-green . . ."

I plunged back to the rail, hung over it, and was sick. Not just once, but again and again, my stomach going on heaving long after there could possibly be anything left in it to bring up. My recollection of the rest of the day, that night, and the following day, is hazy; nor would I wish to remember the time more clearly. At some stage, the French sailor came back with his mixture, and Henry held my head while he poured it down my throat. I think I felt a little better afterward, but I could scarcely have felt worse.

Gradually my state improved. On the fourth morning, although I was still queasy, signs of hunger made themselves known. I washed in salt water, tidied myself up, and made my rolling way toward the galley. The cook, a fat smiling man who prided himself on speaking some English, said, "Ah, so you are better, no? You 'ave recover the good appetite, and prepare to break the fast?"

I smiled. "I think I could manage something."

"Good, good! So we 'ave the special break-the-fast for you. I 'ave cook 'im ready."

He passed me a plate, and I took it. It contained slices of bacon. They were thick, the meat was fat, apart from a couple of narrow bars of pink, and they looked as though they had not been fried but boiled in grease, which still adhered to them. I stared at it, while the cook watched me. Then the ship heaved one way, and my stomach heaved another, and I hurriedly put the plate down and staggered for the fresh air of the deck. As I went, I heard the cook's merry laughter echoing along the companionway behind me.

By the next day, though, I felt perfectly well again. After my enforced privations, my appetite was enormous. The food would have tasted delicious anyway, but in fact it was very good. (The greasy fat bacon, I learned, was an old ship's cook trick; and this one was particularly fond of practical jokes.) Moreover, the weather improved. The seas were still high, but for the most part blue, mirroring skies empty apart from a handful of pelting clouds. The wind stayed fresh, but moved around to the southwest and was less sharp. It was not the best quarter from the point of view of making progress, and a good deal of tacking had to be done to get what advantage we could. Henry and I offered our services, but we were turned down, firmly and courteously. Our inexperienced hands and fumbling fingers would, we realized, be more of a hindrance than a help to them.

So we were thrown back on contemplation of the sea and the sky, and on each other's company. I had noticed a change in Henry on his first return from the Americas, and this had been confirmed during our long ballooning summer. It was not just a physical change, though he was much taller and leaner. There had been a change in his character, too, I thought. He was more reserved, and I felt that might be because he had more in reserve, that he was surer of himself and of his aims in life — aims, that is, quite apart from the one we all shared, of overcoming and destroying the Masters. But we had lived a communal life up in the hills, with little opportunity for or inclination toward confidences. It was only now, in the long days of winter sunshine, with the sea stretching emptily to the four horizons, that he gave me some insight into what the aims might be.

On the rare occasions when I turned my mind to look beyond our primary objective, and thought of the world that could be when it was entirely liberated from our oppressors, my vision was hazy and mostly, I am afraid, centered on pleasures. I envisaged a life of hunting, riding, fishing — all the things which I enjoyed, made a hundred times more enjoyable by the knowledge that no Tripod would ever again stride across the skyline, that we were the masters of our own habitation and destiny, and that any cities that were built would be cities for men to dwell in.

Henry's meditations had been very different. He had been much affected by his first journey across the ocean. He and his companions had landed far to the north of the City on the isthmus, in a land where, as I have said, the people spoke English, though with an unfamiliar accent. He was struck by the fact that there, thousands of miles across trackless seas, he could talk and be understood, whereas when he and I crossed a mere twenty miles of water to France we had found ourselves unable to communicate with those who lived there.

From this, he went on to think more deeply about those divisions of men, which had existed before the Masters came and which the Masters, themselves a single race of one language and nation, had never understood, even though they did not fail to take advantage of them. It seemed to him monstrous that such a state should exist, that men should go out to kill other men they did not know, simply because they lived in a foreign land. This, at any rate, was something that had ceased with the coming of the Masters.

"They brought peace," I agreed, "but what a peace it was! The peace of herded cattle."

"Yes," Henry said. "That's true. But does liberty have to mean slaughtering each other?"

"Men do not fight against each other any

more. We all fight the common enemy — Frenchmen like Beanpole, Germans like Fritz, Americans like your friend Walt . . ."

"*Now* they fight together. But afterward, when we have destroyed the Masters — what will happen then?"

"We shall remain united, of course. We have learned our lesson."

"Are you sure?"

"I am certain! It would be unthinkable for men to go to war with each other again."

He was silent for a few moments. We were leaning against the starboard rail, and far off in the distance I thought I saw something flash, but realized it must be a trick of light. There could be nothing there.

Henry said, "Not unthinkable, Will. I think about it. It must not happen, but we may have to work hard to make sure it does not."

I asked more questions, and he answered them. This, it seemed, was the chief aim he had set himself, of working for the maintenance of peace among the peoples of the free world. I was a little awed by it, but not entirely convinced. There had been war in the past, I knew, but that was because men had never had anything to unite them, as we now had in the struggle against the Masters. Having once gained this unity, it was impossible to imagine that we would ever give it up. Once this war was over . . .

He was saying something, but I interrupted him, grabbing his arm.

"There is something out there. I saw it before, but was not sure. A small flash. Could it be something to do with the Tripods? They can travel on the sea."

"I should be surprised to find them in mid-ocean," Henry said.

He was watching where I pointed. The wink of light came again. He said, "Low down, too, for a Tripod! Not far above the surface of the water. It will be a flying fish, I should think."

"A flying fish?"

"It doesn't really fly. It leaps out of the water, when the dolphins are pursuing it, and glides over the surface, using its fin as a sail. Sometimes they land on board. I believe they're quite good to eat."

"You've seen them before?"

Henry shook his head. "No, but the sailors have told me of them, and of other things. Whales, which are as big as a house, and blow spouts of water up through the tops of their heads, and giant squids, and, in warmer waters, creatures that look like women and suckle their young at the breast. The seas are full of wonders."

I could imagine him listening to their tales. He had become a good listener, attentive to what was being said, courteous and interested. That was another way in which he had changed from the brash thoughtless boy I had known. I realized that if there were any need to keep men together after our victory, Henry was the sort of person who could help to do it. As things stood, Beanpole was becoming important among the scientists, Fritz was acknowledged as one of our best commanders, and even I (chiefly by luck) had had my moments of glory. Henry had been less successful, his one important enterprise a failure, even though through no fault of his own. But it could be that in the world of the future, he would be more valuable than any of us. Even than Beanpole, because what good would it do to rebuild the great-cities of the ancients only to knock them down once more?

Though it was impossible that folly of that sort should happen again.

And, in any case, the Masters were not beaten yet. Not by a long way.

The last stage of our voyage took us through warmer seas. We were heading farther south than on Henry's first voyage, our landfall being close to the secondary base that had been set up in the mountains, some hundred miles east of the City. (It is an odd thing that, although the two continents of the Americas lie north and south of each other, the narrow isthmus that joins them runs east-west.) The primary base, from which the flying machines had been launched, had been abandoned after the failure of the attack. We had steady winds behind us from the northeast, and I was told that these blew, almost without changing, throughout the year. Once we had come under their influence, they propelled us powerfully.

The sea was full of islands, of all shapes and sizes, some tiny and some so enormous that, if the sailors had not kept me better informed, I would have taken them for the continent itself. We sailed quite close to many, and there were tantalizing glimpses of lush green hills, golden sands, feathery fronds of trees waving in a breeze . . . Only the very big ones, it seemed, were inhabited; the Masters had imposed a tabu on the rest, in the minds of the Capped of these parts. It would be wonderful to land and explore them. Perhaps, when this was all over . . . Henry could do his preaching on his own, I decided. I would not have been much use to him, anyway.

We landed at last, and went ashore to feel the unfamiliar solidity of firm ground under our feet. And to realize that we were back in the shadow of the enemy. This took place at dusk, and we unloaded and carted our gear that night, and the following day lay up, in the cover of a forest. The work was difficult, and not helped by the fact than we had to endure several torrential downpours. It was rain unlike any I had encountered before, almost as though solid water were sheeting down out of the sky. It drenched one to the skin within seconds.

In the morning, though, the sun beat hotly down through the leaves of unfamiliar trees. I ventured out to bask and to dry my clothes in a clearing near by. We had already climbed quite high, and this shelf of land looked a long way east. I could see the coastline, with minute offshore islands. Something else, also. It was miles away but clear, pinpointed in the bright tropic light.

A Tripod.

It took us several days to get to our base, and another week to complete our preparations. After that, all we had to do was wait.

I had had to wait before, and thought I had learned patience. There had been the long mouths of training for the Games, the seemingly endless weeks of enforced idleness in the caves, the days by the river preparing for our invasion of the City. All these, I thought, had schooled me; but they had not. For this was waiting of an entirely different kind — waiting with no fixed term and on a permanent alert. We were dependent not on any decisions of men, or even of the Masters, but on the vagaries of a greater force than either, of nature.

Our planning staff, of whom Beanpole was one, had consulted with those, recruited in our earlier expeditions, who had lived here all their lives, and knew the country and its weather. We had to have a wind which would early our balloons over the City, a wind, that is, from the northeast. This was, in fact, the prevailing wind, which had brought us on the last leg of our voyage, and at this time of year, constant. Unfortunately, it normally died out, over this very strip of land, into the equatorial calm which prevailed to the south and west. We must wait for a moment of greater wind strength if we were not to find ourselves becalmed, and even drifting away from our target.

So we had advance positions set up, as near as possible to the City, whose duty was to report back, by pigeon, when the wind was holding strongly enough in that direction. Until they did, we could do nothing but chafe at the delay.

And chafe most of us did. Ours had been the last but one party to arrive, the rest coming a day later, but although many had waited longer, I found myself one of the least able to accept the situation. My temper worsened, and I began flaring up at the smallest provocation. Finally, when one of the others made a joking remark — it was that I was so full of hot air he doubted if I really needed a balloon — I sailed into him, and we fought furiously until we were dragged apart.

That evening, Fritz spoke to me.

We were in a tent but, as was frequently the case, the tent was leaking in several places. The rains of this land were not easily stopped by canvas. It swished down outside as he remonstrated with me. I said I was sorry, but he did not seem much impressed.

"You have been sorry before," he told me, "but you keep on doing things without thinking — flying off the handle. We cannot afford dissension here. We must live together and work together."

"I know," I said. "I will do better." He stared

at me. He was fond of me, I knew, as I of him. We had been together a long time, and shared hardships and dangers. Nevertheless, his expression was grim. He said, "As you know, I am in charge of the attack. Julius and I discussed many things before we left. He told me that if I was not sure of any man I must leave him out of the assault. He spoke of you, Will, in particular."

He liked me, but his duty came first, as it always would with Fritz. I pleaded with him for a last chance. In the end, shaking his head, he said he would — but it really was a last chance. If any trouble occurred in which I was concerned, he would not bother to find out who was responsible. Out I would go.

The following morning, in the course of our usual drill on the balloons, the one I had fought with tripped me — perhaps accidentally, perhaps not — and I went sprawling. Not only did my elbow hit a chunk of rock, but I landed in a patch of sticky mud. I closed my eyes, and lay there for at least five seconds before getting up again. With a smile on my face, and my teeth tightly gritted.

Two mornings later, through yet another downpour, a bedraggled pigeon alighted on the perch in front of its box. A little scroll of paper was fastened to its leg.

We had twelve balloons altogether in our force, with one man to each so as to be able to carry the greatest possible weight of explosive.

This was in the form of metal containers, something like the grooved metal eggs we had found in the ruins of the great-city, but very much larger. It was not too easy a task to lift them over the edge of the basket. They were fitted with fuses, which would cause them to explode four seconds after the release was pulled.

This meant, Beanpole had explained to us, that we needed to make our drop from a height of just under a hundred and fifty feet. The calculation depended on something which had been discovered by a famous scientist of the ancients called Newton. He tried to explain it but it was beyond our comprehension — beyond mine, anyway. What it meant was that an object falling through the air traveled a distance in feet of sixteen, multiplied twice over by the number of seconds it had been falling. Thus in the first second it would fall sixteen feet (sixteen multiplied by one multiplied by one), in two seconds sixty-four feet, and in three a hundred and forty-four. The fourth second was the time allowed for getting the bomb, as he called it, into position and ready for the drop.

We had practiced this with dummy bombs over and over again, learning to calculate distances from the ground, to estimate time, and so on. There was also the question of the forward motion of the balloon, which naturally affected the place at which the bomb dropped. We had become quite skilled in the art. Now we had to apply it.

The balloons went up at two-second intervals into a sodden gray sky and a wind dragging in from the ocean behind us. Our order had been allocated by Fritz, who himself went first. I was sixth, and Henry tenth. As I cast off and found myself shooting skyward, I looked down at the faces so quickly dwindling below. I saw Beanpole looking up, his spectacles almost certainly obscured by rain, but peering through them all the same. It was hard luck on Beanpole, I thought, but the thought was fleeting. I was more concerned with having made it myself, with being freed of all the delays and irritations. The lashing rain had already soaked me, but that was unimportant.

We soared higher, in a long line that still preserved some irregularity. The country on which I looked down was a strange one, made up of low-pointed hills, rounded but in all sorts of different shapes, and covered by the dense forest that stretched away almost to reach the gray line that marked the ocean. The rain drove steadily on the driving wind. Valleys unfolded and folded again behind me. Gradually the hills flattened, and the forests gave way to fields of crops. There were occasional small villages of whitewashed houses. A river appeared, and for a time our course followed it.

The line was breaking up, spreading out, affected by small inconsistencies in the wind. Some balloons were making better progress than others. I was chagrined to find that my own was falling behind. We were in two main groups, nine in advance and three of us forming a rear-guard. Henry was one of the three. I waved to him, and he waved back, but we were not close enough for me to read anything in his face.

We lost the river but found this or another not long after. If it was the same one, it had widened. Later it flowed into a lake, a long neck of water stretching for at least ten miles on our right. The land beneath us was barren and lifeless, with a scorched blackened look. This would be part of the zone all around the City which the Masters had laid waste as a defensive measure. I looked ahead more keenly but saw nothing but water on one side and burned empty land rising on the other. The leading balloons were increasing their lead over us stragglers. It was infuriating, but there was nothing to be done about it.

In fact, we were all traveling more slowly, because the rain had stopped and the wind was less. Our course had been carefully calculated for this wind, but I wondered if the calculation might not be out, or the wind have changed direction, so that we would drift aimlessly out to sea, beyond reach of our target. Ahead, the lake dog-legged to the right. But at that point . . .

It ran south of west, almost straight, absolutely regular, a ditch that the ancients had made to take their great ships across the isthmus from one ocean to the other. There were no ships in it now but there was something else straddling it, a gigantic green-shelled golden beetle. The calculation had not been wrong. Right ahead of us lay the third City of the Masters.

I did not have time to contemplate it. My attention was taken up by something else which appeared from behind high ground to the left of the City. Presumably the Tripod was returning, in the ordinary way, to its base. But, catching sight of the cluster of bubbles bobbing through the air, it checked and changed course. It got to them when the first balloon was within a hundred yards of the Wall. A flailing tentacle came close, but missed, as the balloonist, jettisoning ballast, sent his craft soaring. The others were approaching the Tripod, too. The tentacles flailed again, and this time struck home. The balloon crumpled, and dropped, with its basket, to the dark wet ground below.

The Tripod was like a man swatting insects. Two more balloons in the advance group went down. The others got past. The first was over the City. Something fell from it. I counted: one, two, three . . . nothing happened. The bomb had failed to explode.

Two other balloons were off target, to the left. But the remaining three would cross over the huge expanse of green crystal. Another bomb dropped. Once more I counted. There was a great thump of sound as it went off. But the dome, as far as I could see, was still inviolate. I could not watch what was happening ahead after that. The Tripod stood directly in my path.

Everyone so far had dropped ballast to rise and

dodge the enemy's blows. I guessed he would be getting used to the maneuver. Waiting until the tentacle was moving to its strike, I pulled the release cord and, with a sickening lurch, felt the balloon drop. The tentacle passed overhead. I had no idea by how much, for my attention was on the ground toward which I was falling. Hastily I threw out sandbags, and the balloon shot up. The Tripod was behind me, the City ahead. Glancing back, I saw one of the two last balloons struck down, the other coming on. I hoped that was Henry, but could not look to find out.

I had heard two more explosions, but the City's dome still stood. My balloon was over it and looking down I could dimly see, through its translucent green, the clustered peaks of the pyramids inside. My height was about right, though more by luck than anything else after the evading action I had been forced to take. Reaching down, I pulled out the fuse pin, and heaved the bomb up over the basket's edge, poised it for an instant, and let go.

The balloon lifted with the release of its weight. I counted the seconds. Just before three, it hit, skidded, bounced from the curve of the dome. It went off, and the blast of air rocked me violently. Sick with dismay, I saw that there was no sign of a break in the crystal. That left one single hope, one fragile bubble to crack the mighty carapace of the aliens.

It was Henry. I knew that by the color of the

shirt he was wearing. He was going in dead center over the City. But not keeping the height that Beanpole and the scientists had prescribed I watched him dropping, dropping . . . The basket scraped the surface of the dome.

Then I understood what he was about. He had seen the failure of those of us in front and understood the reason for it. The scientists had told us that the bombs were powerful enough to shatter the crystal, having experimented on the broken dome of the City we had taken, but of course the bomb had to be touching or very close to the crystal when the explosion took place. Our bombs had ricocheted enough to be outside those limits, and the odds were against his being any more successful. That was as far as dropping the bomb was concerned.

But *planting* was another matter. My own transit had been toward the edge, with the roof a falling curve beneath me. But Henry had been lucky enough to go in across the center. So huge was the dome's expanse that a man might walk across it without difficulty.

My mind was full of hope, and horror. The basket scraped again, bounced up, dropped. I saw the small distant figure struggle to lift something. I wanted to shout to him to let it go — that it would probably stay where it fell or at any rate merely slide down the slight curve, staying in contact — but it would have done no good. As I watched, he scrambled over the edge of the basket. The balloon, released, rose sharply into the sullen gray sky. Henry stayed there, crouching, antlike against the gleaming vastness that stretched all around.

Crouching, and cradling something in his arms.

I turned away. Not until some seconds after the explosion did I have the heart to look back. The Masters' air billowed up like green smoke from a ragged hole which, as I looked, crumbled still farther at the edges.

Almost blindly I pulled the cord and let my balloon drop to the waiting earth.

9

The Conference of Man

Once before three of us had gone up through the tunnel that climbed inside the mountain to the fields of eternal snow and ice at the top. We had walked then, resting when we were tired, lighting our way with the big slow-burning tallow candles which were used to illuminate the lower caves in which we lived. Not quite the same three. Fritz took the place that had been Henry's.

And not in the same way, either. Instead of walking we sat at ease in one of the four carriages pulled by the small but powerful diesel-electric train up the cogged track. Instead of the dim flicker of candlelight we were in a bright and even radiance, in which one could read a book if one had a mind to. We did not carry rations — tough stringy dried meat and hard tasteless biscuits — because food was to be provided at our journey's end, where a skilled staff of fifty waited, more than eleven thousand feet above the sea, to look after the delegates and those fortunate others who had been invited to attend the Conference of Man.

It was Julius's wish that it should be held here, high up among the peaks of the White Mountains that had sheltered the early seeds of man's resistance to his conquerors. It was by Julius's order that we, along with other survivors of the days of battle, had come. We were not delegates, though probably we could have been had we so desired. I am not boasting in saying that. It was just that those of us who had fought against the Masters and defeated them could claim privileges everywhere . . . and had so wearied of adulation that we preferred to look for quietness and privacy.

The three of us had looked in different directions. Beanpole was immersed in research in the vast laboratories that had been built in France, not far from the castle by the sea. Fritz had turned farmer in his own native land, and spent his days with his crops and beasts. While I, more restless and perhaps less purposeful than they, had sought peace in exploring those parts of the world which the Masters had stripped of their previous human inhabitants. In a ship, with half a dozen others, I crossed the seas, and put in to strange forgotten harbors on unknown coasts. Under sail because, although there were ships now with engines, we preferred it that way.

This had been our first meeting in two years. We had laughed and talked a lot when we met, in the town that lay between two lakes down in the valley, but the talk had dried up during the long journey inside the mountain. We were engaged with our own thoughts. Mine were somewhat melancholy. I was remembering the things we had done together, the times we had had. It would have been pleasant to preserve that comradeship in the days that came after. Pleasant, but alas, impossible. That which had brought us together had gone, and now our paths diverged, according to our natures and our needs. We would meet again, from time to time, but always a little more as strangers; until perhaps at last, as old men with only memories left, we could sit together and try to share them.

Because with victory everything had changed. There had been the months of anxious waiting for the arrival of the great ship of the Masters, but even during that time the world had been picking itself up, relearning forgotten skills, compressing into months what it had taken our forefathers decades, centuries even, to accomplish. Only when, one autumn night, a new star winked in the sky did people pause to draw breath, and stare anxiously out into the heavens.

It was a star that moved, a point of light traveling past the fixed familiar ones. In powerful telescopes it resolved into a shape, a metal cocoon. Scientists made calculations of its size, and the result was breathtaking. More than a mile long, they said, and a quarter of a mile wide at its thickest part. It swung in an orbit round the earth and we waited, tense, to see what it would do, finding no answer come to the radio messages that it was sending to its colonists.

They had won that first time by guile, and the trick would not work twice. The air of our planet was poison to them, and they had no base in which to shelter. Men still wore Caps, but the Caps would give no orders. They could try to set up fresh bases, and they might succeed, but we would harry them continually with weapons that were more and more sophisticated every year. Having beaten them when they were all powerful and we pitifully weak, we knew we could better any effort they made in the future.

Alternatively they could cast down death and destruction from their secure haven in the skies. This was a possibility to which many inclined, and which I myself thought most likely, at the beginning at least. They might hope that after a long enough time of this we would be so weakened, our spirit so shattered, that they could then descend and hope to rule our battered and blackened planet. That would be a longer struggle, and a crueler one, but we would win that, too, in the end.

They did neither. They merely sent down three bombs, and each landed on its target and destroyed it utterly. The targets were the dead Cities of their colonists. We lost the men who were working in them at the time, including many scientists, but it was a loss of a few hundred when it might have been millions. And when the third bomb had exploded, the light in the sky suddenly dwindled, and disappeared. At the instant that it did so, Ruki, the last of the Masters left alive on earth, stirred in his prison cell — a new one, well appointed, with a high ceiling, and a garden pool, and a plate glass front through which men could watch him like a beast in a zoo — howled once, crumpled, and died.

The train chugged through the last of the intermediate stations, and the walls of the tunnel closed in around us again. I said, "Why did they give in so easily? I have never really understood."

Fritz looked puzzled, but perhaps Beanpole's thoughts had been running in the same channel as my own. He said, "I don't think anyone knows. I read a new book about them recently, by the man who was in charge of studying Ruki during those final months. They know a lot about the way their bodies worked, from the dissections, but their minds are still very largely a mystery. They resigned themselves to fate, somehow, in a way that men do not. Those in the Tripods died when their Cities did. Ruki gave up the ghost when he knew, in some strange way, that the ship had abandoned him and turned back into the deeps of space. I do not think we shall ever know how it happens."

"Perhaps we shall meet them again," I said. "How are the plans for the rocket to the moon progressing?"

"Well," Beanpole said. "And so is the work on the flame-energy they used. It is a form of atomic power, but much more subtle than that which the ancients developed. We shall be out among the stars within a hundred years, perhaps within fifty."

"Not I," I said cheerfully. "I shall stick to my tropic seas."

Fritz said, "If we do meet them again out there . . . it will be their turn to fear *us*."

The Conference Hall had huge windows along one side, through which one looked out onto a dozen or more mountain peaks, white with snow, and onto the great river of imperceptibly moving ice which ran for thirty miles among them. The sun stood in a cloudless sky above it all. Everything was sharp and dazzling; so bright that one needed dark glasses to look out for more than a moment or two.

In the Hall, the Council, with Julius presiding, sat at a table at one end, on a dais only slightly raised from the level of the rest of the floor. Most of the rest of the space was taken up by the delegates' seats. At the far end, behind a silken rope barrier, was the place for the rest of us. Those, like ourselves, who had come on the Council's special invitation, certain officials, and representatives of the newspapers and the radio stations. (In a year or two, we had been promised, there would be something called television, by which men could see, in their own homes, things happening half a world away. It was the device which the Masters had used, as a preliminary stage in their conquest, to hypnotize men and so control their minds — and our scientists were making sure that could not happen again before they brought it back.)

The room, although large and high-ceilinged, was very crowded. We had seats at the front of our section, and so looked directly onto the benches of the delegates, which were arranged in concentric circles around a small central space. Each section had the sign of the country from which they came. I saw the name of my own land, England, the names of France, Germany, Italy, Russia, the United States of America, China, Egypt, Turkey . . . one could not take them all in.

From a door at the other end, the members of the Council began to file in and take their places at the table on the dais. We all rose as they did so. Julius came last, limping heavily on his stick, and applause swelled in a sea of sound around the room. When it died at last, the Secretary of the Council, a man called Umberto, spoke. He was brief. He announced the opening of the Conference of Man, and called on the President of the Council to speak.

There was more applause, which Julius checked with a slight gesture of his hand. It was two years since I had seen him, also. He did not seem to have changed much. A little more bent, perhaps, but there was vigor in his attitude, and his voice was strong.

He wasted no time on talk of the past. What concerned us was the present, and the future. Our scientists and technologists were rapidly re-acquiring the knowledge and skills of our ancestors, and even improving on them. The promise of all this was inestimable. But the glorious future which man could and should enjoy depended also on the way in which he governed himself, for man was the measure of all things.

A glorious future . . . It was right, I thought, for Julius to speak in that strain, because there was no doubt that, in doing so, he spoke for the overwhelming majority of the peoples of the world. They had an insatiable appetite for the toys and wonders of the past. Everywhere one went, in so-called civilized lands, one heard radio, and there was great impatience for television. I had visited my parents on my way here, and had heard my father talk about installing electricity at the mill. In Winchester, new buildings had started to soar within a stone's throw of the cathedral.

It was what most people wanted, but I did not. I thought of the world into which I had been born, and in which I had grown up — the world of villages and small towns, of a peaceful ordered life, untroubled, unhurried, taking its pattern from the seasons. I thought, too, of my stay at the Château de la Tour Rouge, of the Comte and Comtesse, of the days of riding and sitting idly in the sun, of summer meadows, trout-filled streams, of the squires talking and laughing together, the knights jousting in the tournament . . . And of Eloise. Her face, small and calm and lovely under the blue turban, was as clear as though it were only yesterday that I had awakened from my fever, and seen her looking down at me. No, the fine new world that was being built held few attractions for me. Fortunately, I was able to turn my back on it, and find my way through empty seas into faraway harbors.

Julius was continuing to talk about government. This was the crucial thing, and all else flowed from it. The Council had been formed in the days when a handful of men hid in caves and plotted the recovery of the world's freedom. That freedom had been achieved, and local governments had arisen, all over the world, each administering its own territory. International affairs, the control of science, and so on, fell into the jurisdiction of the Council.

It was clearly in the interests of everyone that some such system should continue. But it was also essential that it should come under the democratic control of the peoples of the world. For this reason, the Council was prepared to dissolve itself and hand over its authority and functions to a similar, though possibly larger, body which would be properly representative. This would require study and organization, and there must be a further transitional period for this. The Conference should decide the length of time required. The Conference also should appoint the new provisional Council to take the place of the present one.

"I think that is all I need to say," Julius said. "All that remains is for me to thank you all for your cooperation in the past, and to wish good fortune to the new Council, and the new President."

He sat down to a renewed outbreak of applause. It was loud and enthusiastic but, I could see, surprisingly patchy. There were even some who sat with folded hands. As it died away, someone rose, and the Secretary, who was acting as Speaker, said, "I call on the senior delegate from Italy."

He was a short swarthy man, with hair growing in a scanty halo around the mesh of the Cap. He said, "I propose, before anything else, the reelection of Julius as President of the new Council."

There were cheers, but not from all the delegates.

The senior German delegate said, "I second that motion."

There were cries of "Vote!" but others of denial. In the confusion, someone else rose and was recognized. I recognized him, too, as a man I remembered. It was Pierre, who had spoken against Julius those six long years ago in the caves. He was a delegate of France.

He began to speak calmly, but I thought there was something else not far beneath the calm, something much more violent. He attacked first of all the procedure that was being suggested, of appointing a new President first. This should follow the formation of a new Council, not precede it. He went on to speak against the suggestion that there should be a further transitional period with the Council a provisional body. There was no need for this. The Conference had the power to create a fully effective and permanent Council, and should do so. We had wasted enough time already.

He paused and then, looking directly at Julius, went on, "It is not only a matter of wasting time. Gentlemen, this Conference has been brought here to be used. It was known in advance that certain delegates would propose the reappointment of Julius as President. We are expected, out of sentiment, to vote him back into office. We are asked to confirm a despot in power."

Shouting and uproar followed. Pierre waited until it had quieted, and said, "At times of crisis, it may be necessary to accept the rule of one man, of a dictator. But the crisis is over. The world we create must be a democratic world. And we ourselves cannot give way to sentiment or to any other weakness. We are sent here to represent the people, to serve their interests."

The Italian delegate called, "Julius saved us all."

"No," Pierre said, "that is not true. There were others who worked and fought for freedom — hundreds, thousands of others. We accepted Julius as our leader then, but that is no reason for accepting him now. Look at this Conference. The Council has taken long enough to summon it. The authority they have was given to them until such a time as the Masters were utterly defeated. That happened nearly three years ago, but only now, reluctantly . . ."

There was a new disturbance, out of which the German delegate could be heard saying, "It was not possible before. There has had to be much readjustment . . .”

Pierre cut through his words, “And why here? There are dozens, a hundred places in the world better suited to hold such a Conference as this. We are here on the whim of an aging tyrant. Yes, I insist! Julius wanted the Conference held here, among the peaks of the White Mountains, as yet another means of reminding us of the debt we are supposed to owe him. Many delegates are from low-lying lands and find conditions here oppressive. Several have been ill with mountain sickness and have been forced to go down to the lower levels. This does not bother Julius. He has brought us to the White Mountains, thinking that here we will not dare to vote against him. But if men care for their freedom, he will find he is wrong.”

Shouts and countershouts echoed across the Hall. One of the American delegates made a strong quiet speech in Julius's support. So did a Chinese delegate. But others followed Pierre's line. A delegate from India declared that personalities were unimportant. What mattered was the building of strong and vigorous government, and that required a strong and vigorous leader. And one not enfeebled by age. Julius had done great things and would long be remembered. But his place now should be taken by a younger man.

Fritz, beside me, said, “They will vote him out.”

“They can't,” I said. “It is unthinkable. A few

are yapping, but when it comes to a vote . . ."

The debate dragged on. The vote came at last, on the motion to reappoint Julius as President. They had rigged up an electrical device, by which delegates pressed buttons marked "For" or "Against," and the results were recorded on a screen set in the rear wall. The huge figures lit up.

For: 152.

I held my breath. Against . . .

Against: 164.

The storm that followed, made up of cheers and shouts of indignation, was more violent than any of the previous ones. It did not end until it could be seen that Julius was on his feet. He said, "The Conference has made its decision." He looked no different, his expression was composed, but his voice suddenly was very tired. "We must all accept it. I ask only that we remain united under whatever President and Council are appointed. Men do not count. Unity does."

The applause this time was scattered. The senior delegate from the United States said, "We came here in good faith, prepared to work with men of all nations. We have heard petty bickering, abuse of a great man. The history books told us that this was what Europeans were like, that they could never change, but we did not believe them. Well, we believe them now. This delegation hereby withdraws from this farce of a Conference. We have a continent of our own, and can look after ourselves."

They picked up their things and headed for the door. Before they had got there, a Chinese delegate, in his soft lilting voice, said, "We agree with the American delegation. We do not feel our interests will be served by a Council dominated by the passions which have been shown today. Regretfully, we must depart."

One of the German delegates said, "This is the work of the French. They are concerned only with their own interests and ambitions. They wish to dominate Europe as they dominated it in the past. But I would say to them: beware. We Germans have an army which will defend our frontiers, an air force . . ."

His remarks were lost in pandemonium. I saw the English delegates stand up and move, in silent disgust, to follow those who had already left. I looked at Julius. His head was bowed, his hands over his eyes.

From the Conference building you could walk out, over hard-packed snow, up the slope to the Jungfraujoch itself. The Jungfrau glistened on our left, the Mönch and Eiger on our right. There was the rounded dome of the observatory, once more in use to study the distant passionless heavens. Below us, snowfields plunged away and one could see down into the green valley. The sun was setting, and it was in shadow.

We had been silent since we came up from the hill. Now Beanpole said, "If Henry had not died . . ."

I said, "Would one man have made any difference?"

"One man might. Julius did. And it could have been more than one. I would have helped him, if he had wanted me to."

I thought about that. I said, "Perhaps I would also. But Henry's dead."

Fritz said, "I think perhaps I will give up my farming. There are things more important."

Beanpole said, "I'm with you."

Fritz shook his head. "It is different for you. Your work is important, mine not."

"Not as important as this," Beanpole said. "What about you, Will? Are you ready for a new fight — a longer, less exciting one, with no great triumphs at the end? Will you leave your seas and islands, and help us try to get men to live together, in peace as well as liberty? An Englishman, a German, and a Frenchman: it would be a good start."

The air was cold but exhilarating. A gust of wind scattered powdery snow from the face of the Jungfrau.

"Yes," I said, "I'll leave my seas and islands."

We hope you have enjoyed this Large Print book. Other G.K. Hall & Co. or Chivers Press Large Print books are available at your library or directly from the publishers.

For more information about current and upcoming titles, please call or write, without obligation, to:

All our Large Print titles are designed for easy reading, and all our books are made to last.